HIDDEN HOLLYWOOD

KYLIE GILMORE

Amy,
Join the club and
get your happy
ending!
Kylie

This book is a work of fiction. Names, characters, places, brands, media, and incidents are the product of the author's imagination or are used fictitiously. The author acknowledges the trademarked status and trademark owners of various products referenced in this work of fiction, which have been used without permission. The publication/use of these trademarks are not authorized, associated with, or sponsored by the trademark owners. Any resemblance to actual events, locales, or persons, living or dead, is purely coincidental.

First Edition: October 2016
Cover design by Kim Killion
Published by: Extra Fancy Books

ISBN-10: 1-942238-24-X
ISBN-13: 978-1-942238-24-9

Because a romance book club would rock...

CHAPTER ONE

Claire Jordan went by a lot of names—hottest actress under thirty, sexiest woman alive, Duck Lips (that was her brother)—but she'd yet to be called, um, slut. At least, not to her face.

She stifled a laugh as she sat in the circle of seven women gathered in the private executive lounge of the luxury hotel in New York City that was her temporary home. The twentysomething women had formed a singles book club, but after months of no men joining them, they were now debating a more fitting name. Mad (short for Madison) Campbell, a petite badass with short purple dyed hair, had suggested "SLUTS," and a spirited debate over the pros and cons ensued.

Claire didn't comment, she was a temporary member, but she sure as hell enjoyed the show. And it distracted the leader of the book club, Hailey Adams, from her mission to get Claire out on a date. The woman, an ambitious wedding planner/matchmaker with a heart of gold, was appalled at Claire's year-long break from men. Claire had good reason, plus the rumors that the onscreen chemistry between her and her costar had carried over to real life were crucial to the buzz for her movie. She'd sunk everything she had into producing the Fierce trilogy movies. She couldn't afford a huge marketing campaign on top of that. The temporary pleasure of a date would never be worth the risk of losing all that free press or, worse, dealing with bad press before the release next year. So what if the ache of loneliness sometimes made it hard to breathe? That was the price she paid to live her dream.

Mad straightened out of her usual slouch and lifted her chin. "What's wrong with Super Lovers of Underrated Terrific Stories?"

Hailey tossed her long strawberry blonde hair over one shoulder and barked, "For the last time, we are not calling ourselves SLUTS!"

A sly expression crossed Mad's face as she tapped her finger against her lips. Her black T-shirt, ripped down the center in a small V, read Try Me. What Claire wouldn't give to be more like Mad—enjoying not giving a fuck. Claire always had to be protective of her image. Something she'd learned the hard way on more than one occasion. Now she didn't let anyone close enough to damage her rep or her heart.

"We need something with good energy," another

woman said. "We're a romance book club. Something with love."

The other women agreed and chatted quietly to each other about the possibilities. Claire remained silent. It was late September and she'd only be filming *Fierce Longing*, based on the bestselling novel by book club member Julia Marino, for two more months. Then she'd be onto the next project. Life of an actor. It was rare for the friendships forged on location to continue. Sure, she'd see some of the crew on the next movie she produced, if they were available, but for the most part the people in her life changed with each film.

Mad smiled widely, leaning forward in her enthusiasm, revealing a small hawk tattoo above her heart. "Superb Lovers in Triumphant Stories."

Hailey went nearly apoplectic in her seat, her pale skin flushing, before she caught Mad's smug expression. Then she composed herself enough to say, "Sure, Mad. We'd love to be called SLITS."

Mad went for the kill. "Complete Lovers In Te—"

"No!" Hailey shouted, leaping from her seat. She looked around, seeming surprised to find herself standing.

"Mad, you devil," Claire said with a grin.

Mad snickered.

Hailey nodded once at Claire and regained her

composure, returning to her seat and smoothing the front of her blue dress. Hailey was the only one dressed up. Claire wore her casual outfit—a black silk blouse with black jeans and bright orange Gucci pumps. Even in her downtime, she still had to look photo ready just in case. Her new friends hadn't even asked for a selfie with her, something she was sure was Hailey's doing. Hailey had made it possible for Claire to attend Julia's wedding three months ago in Clover Park, Connecticut, with impressive discretion from the security detail to the gentle handling of guests, who were not permitted to share images or stories of Claire. Amazing really, considering there were a hundred guests and not one of them signed a nondisclosure. Of course, the paparazzi had hovered nearby the mansion where the wedding and reception were held, but not one picture or story on Claire from *inside* the mansion had appeared anywhere. That was the power of Hailey. Keeping Claire's privacy within a small book club was a stroll in the park after that. Besides, Claire already trusted Julia because they were equally invested in the Fierce trilogy. The other women had grown on her quickly over the past month with their warmth and good humor, and none of them had breathed a word about Claire.

Julia had been the one to invite Claire and had arranged for the book club to meet in the private lounge, a bland space done in muted gray with white sofas and plush white chairs, instead of Claire's penthouse suite, to help the other women "focus on the real you." Claire didn't mind. She rarely let anyone into her private space. Julia was a total sweetheart, smoothing things over at that first awkward meeting and assuring everyone that Claire was a bookworm just like them. She'd met the book club briefly at the wedding, where they'd been starstruck, but that passed quickly at her first book club meeting when Claire snorted iced tea out her nose over something Mad said. Claire hadn't always been glam. It was a part she played like any other.

"Smut book club!" another woman exclaimed. "We do like smutty stories."

A sweet woman in glasses added in a throaty purr, "I read for *pleasure*."

Everyone cracked up.

It was Julia who finally came up with the winning turn of phrase. She was the writer, after all. "The Happy Endings Book Club. We all love a happy ending, right? And it's a little wink at the other kind of happy ending."

"I'm all about hot sex," Mad said seriously. "I barely read at all until I found *Fierce Longing*."

Julia blushed, bright pink dotting her cheeks. She lifted her long brown hair off her neck. "Thank you."

"You've got one dirty mind," Mad said appreciatively.

Julia's blush spread to her neck. "Thanks," she muttered, dropping her hair and fidgeting in her seat.

"I never woulda guessed it of ya," Mad said, seeming to enjoy making Julia squirm. Julia was a true introvert and, sadly, a monster blusher. Her color crept into the red zone as Mad waved up and down Julia's body. "What with that whole girl-next-door thing you've got going on. Barely any skin showing—"

"It's settled!" Hailey announced. "The Happy Endings Book Club. Any objections?" She pointed her pink fingernail at each of them in turn, and finding no objections, she beamed. "Okay! Happy Endings Book Club members, our next book will be…"

The women leaned in.

"*Gone with the Wind*!" Hailey exclaimed. "And we can watch the movie after we read it."

The women seemed pleased with this choice. As the room quieted, Hailey's gaze landed on Claire, and Claire did her best to play it cool. Any pause in the action always seemed to remind Hailey that Claire really needed to get back into the dating game. She'd remained fixated on Claire, she was sure, in the hopes of ultimately planning a big celebrity wedding. Claire tread carefully and politely, she didn't want things to get awkward at book club. She knew Hailey had good intentions, and Claire really needed this girl-bonding time in her life.

Mad delayed the inevitable Hailey prodding by producing a bottle of tequila from her canvas messenger bag. "Maybe book club is ready to branch out a bit from books." She took a slug, wiped the rim with her sleeve, and passed it to Julia, who did likewise. The bottle made its way around the circle of women. Claire took a healthy swig, wiped the rim, and passed it to Hailey. She loved that they all drank from the same bottle. Like they were spit sisters.

The conversation got loud and raunchy after that. The women swapped stories on the worst sex they'd had with sloppy kissers, fumblers, and one-minute wonders. Claire kept her mouth shut because her boyfriends were recognizable names. Gorgeous, chiseled male perfection with big wallets and big egos. And shriveled cold hearts. Mad passed the tequila bottle back to Claire, and after another healthy swig, she found herself admitting, "Men just want bragging rights they've been with Claire Jordan. They don't care about me." She swallowed over the lump in her throat. "At all."

The women fell silent, their gazes sympathetic, and she realized she'd said too much. She was at the top of her game, the elite tier of Hollywood that so few ever reached, and had absolutely nothing to complain about. "I mean…" Damn, she'd just depressed the hell out of herself admitting the truth. Men used her.

"If only they could all be like Damon," Mad said, breaking the awkward silence. That was the hero of the Fierce trilogy. She turned to Julia. "I can't believe you made him up. Why can't he be real?"

Julia blushed. "I'm sure there's a Damon out there for all of you."

Doubtful. Since Damon was actually Julia's husband, Angel. Claire was one of the few people who knew this fact, having picked up on it at her first meeting with them. Julia had sworn her to secrecy and got it in writing. Claire found it all supremely romantic.

Hailey's voice rang out, firm and confident. "Claire, I can help you."

Claire straightened, suddenly wary even in her buzzed state. The moment she'd been dreading ever since, well, since she'd discovered the leader of the book club had motivations beyond sharing a love of books.

"Here we go!" Mad exclaimed.

The women tittered. Hailey's serious *I mean business* face was a little funny—the l-o-o-ove business. Two swigs of tequila made it tough for Claire to keep a straight face. Hailey's business card had silver embossed bells and read Hailey Adams, Love Junkie, for crying out loud! *Not funny, not funny.*

Hailey pinned Claire with a determined look. "It's no secret that you've been with Hollywood royalty. And I think you'd enjoy a regular date with a regular guy."

Claire cocked her head and got a little dizzy. This was new. Usually Hailey just urged Claire to get back out there. She'd never been so specific. She wondered who the regular guy was and what he did that was so regular.

Before she could ask, Mad piped up. "How do you expect her to do that? She can barely leave the hotel without starting a riot."

Reality hit. In her tequila-soaked happy place, she'd been thinking impossible things, like she could actually have a regular date as her old irreverent down-to-earth regular self. Did that person even exist anymore? Some part of her feared she'd played the glamorous Claire Jordan so long she might've lost herself.

"I'm super busy, Hailey," Claire said politely, ending the date conversation. "Thanks, though."

"Are you still off on Monday?" Hailey asked as if Claire hadn't just *ended the conversation.* "I'm thinking a hike with a picnic."

Hailey knew Claire's schedule because the women worked around it for their book club meetings, which

Claire was humbled and grateful for. She put in long hours as producer, director, and lead actress on the Fierce movies through her production company Red Jewel Films. Claire bit back a sigh. This was a dangerous idea, even if she secretly longed for something as normal as a hike with a picnic. Some of her favorite memories were of camping in North Carolina when her dad was stationed there for the army. Still, Hailey had to realize this plan had a ton of flaws in it.

"Impossible," Claire stated with great finality. *Ending the conversation.*

Julia spoke up. "A disguise could work. It's just like those stories when someone royal wants to feel what it's like among the commoners."

Claire shot Julia a dark look for encouraging Hailey. "That's not fair to my date. What if he actually liked the person in disguise and then it turns out to be a lie?" That was what happened in all those princess and peasant stories. And, boy, would that guy be pissed and likely take his revenge out in the press. She'd barely recovered from the last PR nightmare that had soured her on men. Last year she had to take her egocentric manwhore ex to court for taking nude pictures of her when she was sleeping (after mediocre sex) and selling them to the highest trashy bidder. She suppressed a shudder at the memory. The risk of exposure would never be worth any picnic.

Hailey framed a dreamy vision in the air like *she* was the director. "Picture this. You're in disguise as regular girl Jenny Coleman. I suggest a redheaded wig. Josh has a thing for redheads." She flushed bright pink. "He once told me that."

Claire clamped her mouth shut over the natural question that sprang to mind. *Who's Josh?* It didn't matter who Josh was because this date was *not happening.* And too bad about the redhead thing because she was a brunette for this movie. Normally she was blonde.

"You're a redhead," Julia said to Hailey.

"She's strawberry blond," Mad said in a chirpy impersonation of Hailey. The women snickered. She really did sound like Hailey.

Hailey shot Mad a quelling look, which Mad responded to by blowing her a kiss.

"Thanks, but no thanks," Claire said firmly. She could already see the headlines that would ruin her movie buzz—Claire Jordan splits with costar Blake Grenier to sneak off in disguise with secret lover! Damon and Mia break up! (Damon and Mia were their characters' names in the Fierce movies, and they still had two more to film.) Or some catchier but equally damaging headline.

She'd never get to have normal. The book club was

as close as she'd get. She got all mushy, taking in her new friends. Their friendship over the last month meant so much to her. They eased the empty ache of loneliness she used to desperately try to fill with parties and work and shiny people. She was saved from the dopey, "I love you, guys," on the tip of her tongue when Hailey ordered, "Someone pass the tequila to Claire."

The nearly empty bottle made its way around the circle to her.

"Eat the worm," Hailey said.

Claire stared at the curled-up disgusting worm at the bottom of the bottle. What kind of crap tequila was this anyway? She'd never seen a worm in the tequila bottles at any of the parties she'd been to. Must be some kind of off brand.

"You eat the worm," Claire returned.

A rare silence fell over the usually chatty group.

Hailey's blue eyes held a challenge. "Eat the worm and I'll drop the date thing." It suddenly occurred to Claire that Hailey wasn't all pink fluff and determined cheer. There were claws.

Claire had never backed down from a challenge. She grabbed a nearby empty water glass, poured the tequila out, and snagged the worm with two fingers. Someone gasped.

It was so mushy. She felt queasy.

Hailey narrowed her eyes.

Claire tilted her head back, opened her mouth, and—

Threw it at Hailey.

Unfortunately she missed and it landed on the floor in front of Hailey, who scooped it up and stood, holding it high in the air. "Behold the worm of fate!"

"Eat it, eat it," Mad chanted.

Hailey threw it at Mad, who quickly tossed it at Julia. The women shrieked as the worm got tossed around like a gross potato before it finally landed on Charlotte, a personal trainer, who had no qualms about picking it up and tossing it in the trash.

"The worm of fate is heading to the dump," Claire said with a laugh, hoping that was the end of this date nonsense. The women laughed along with her, except for Hailey, who looked determined to help Claire.

"Chill," Mad said to Hailey. "Geez, you look like a nutty general staring her down like that. You can't make someone go on a date. It's a free country."

Hailey's gaze never faltered.

Claire grabbed the water glass with tequila and took a swig. "So your plan is to send me into the woods alone with some strange guy?" she asked in the tone of *duh, serial killer.*

"It's not some strange guy," Hailey said. "It's Josh."

Claire's natural curiosity won out. "Who's Josh?"

"Mad's older brother," Hailey said, hitching a thumb at Mad. "Actually I don't know if that's a selling point."

"Ooh! Dagger to the heart!" Mad exclaimed, miming a knife to her heart and then making dramatic, jerky death throes before collapsing to the floor.

The women applauded. Claire too. Mad lifted her head with a grin.

"Ha-ha," Hailey said. "Mad, please don't tell Josh who Claire really is."

"Why would I do that?" Mad asked. "Claire's my friend." She raised a fist, leaned over, and gave Claire a fist bump.

"Because he's your brother," Hailey said in an exasperated voice.

Mad rolled her eyes. "Hey, if he wants to go on a bunch of blind dates set up by you for the idiotic reason of making you jealous, then he deserves what he gets."

"That's ridiculous," Hailey said, smoothing her hair. "Josh and I have an understanding. He's part of my business plan."

"Moron." Mad stood. "Excuse me while I take a wiz."

"My Lord, it's like she was raised by wolves,"

Hailey muttered.

"Just about," Mad said and headed to the private bathroom on the far side of the lounge.

Hailey gestured for Claire to come closer. Claire shook her head and got woozy. She might've had a swig too many with her spit sisters.

Hailey huffed. "Fine! I'll tell everyone. I've never had any complaints from the women Josh takes out. They all say he's a perfect gentleman and never makes a move." She paused, a puzzled expression on her face. "That's weird, isn't it? Now that I think about it. Why doesn't he make a move?"

"Maybe he's gay," Charlotte said, stretching out her long legs. "All the hot ones are." She turned to Claire. "He's a bartender at Garner's back in Clover Park. Majorly hot."

Hailey flushed. "No, he's definitely not gay." Her brow furrowed as she continued the conversation with herself. "Not one of those women ever appealed enough to make a move? Unlikely. I'd better call and find out what's up with that." She grabbed her purse and headed out of the lounge.

Claire suspected there might be something to Mad's theory that Josh only took the women out to make Hailey jealous. That would explain why he kept the date platonic. Besides, if he was majorly hot, why would he need to go on blind dates at all?

Claire took that opportunity to get the bag she'd stashed behind the bar with all the signed *Fierce Longing* books. She headed to the table on the far side of the room and stacked all the books. "I brought you ladies a present. Signed by me and Blake. After Julia signs them as Catherine Cliff, they're all yours." That was Julia's pen name.

The women cheered.

Julia beamed. "Let me get a pen."

"This is so cool!" Charlotte exclaimed. "The trifecta! Ladies, keep your signed book in a safe place. It's going to be worth millions one day."

Claire smiled. Doubtful. But it would be a very special memento of their brief time together. She snagged a book for herself. "I want you all to sign mine."

Mad returned a few minutes later and grabbed a book for herself, peeking in at the signatures. "Awesome. Thanks, Claire."

"You're welcome," Claire said. "Make sure you sign mine. It's making the rounds."

"You're okay," Mad said with a big smile.

Her heart squeezed, her eyes suddenly stinging with unshed tears. "You too," she managed.

Hailey returned, cell phone in hand, and stopped next to Claire to announce, "He says the sex is free, but they have to ask him. He wants a clear affirmation of desire and consent." She flushed bright pink. "So that's the deal. That's nice, I think."

"Oh my God," Charlotte exclaimed. "He seriously said that?"

Claire had no idea what to say to that. She stared at Hailey blankly.

Hailey cleared her throat and then coughed. "Those were his exact words."

A disturbing thought suddenly occurred to Claire. "Wait. The sex is free? What isn't free?"

"Uh…" Hailey looked around like someone else might answer.

"Did you offer to *pay* him to take me out?" Claire asked, incredulous. Not only was this a setup, but Hailey had to pay the guy to take her out? Unbelievable!

Hailey put her hand reassuringly on Claire's arm. "He's the warm-up guy. I have to give him some incentive." She smiled brightly. "Anyway, you'll like him. I'm sure you'll be thanking me later."

Julia looked up. "I'd give Josh my book club stamp of approval." She stamped the table with an imaginary stamper.

The women all followed suit, stamping an imaginary stamp in their palm. Even Mad.

Book club approved.

Claire slumped in her seat. She could have anyone.

There was no door closed to her.

Except for the door with a regular-guy date behind it. Could she really have a little fun adventure and no one would get hurt? She missed being her old self, missed not worrying about what she said or how she looked. And she really missed moving freely without the paparazzi, enjoying nature. She looked up to find the women all smiling encouragingly at her. She so wanted to say yes.

No, it was impossible. She was tequila dreaming. The rational part of herself knew better. She could never have the regular-girl experience and definitely not with a paid escort.

"I can't go out with someone paid to be with me," she finally said, and the women sighed in disappointment. "You see how that could look bad if it got out?"

Hailey worried her bottom lip. "I'll see if I can work something out. No, I know I can. Don't worry, Claire, I'll take care of everything."

Claire rubbed her forehead. Two (or was it three?) swigs of tequila made thinking tough. "Let me think it over."

Mad produced a second bottle of tequila from her bag—no worm in this one—and started a game of "Never Have I Ever" that had them rolling on the floor. Because Mad had done some weird-ass things—

setting up plastic pink flamingos on the principal's front lawn, dressing up like Darth Vader for prom, disguising herself as a boy and kicking ass on the Police Athletic League's baseball team. At the time, they'd wanted girls to stick to softball. She was tough and smart and Claire had a bit of a girl crush. Not the sexy kind, just the let's hang out kind. And because she liked Mad so much, she was warming to the idea of a fun date with her brother. Sight unseen.

Yikes! She must've had too much to drink.

Finally, it was late and they were all fighting back yawns. They said their goodbyes. Everyone left with a signed book, and Claire had her own signed memento clutched to her chest to ward off the returning ache of loneliness as she watched the group leave without her. The women chatted; occasionally one would grab the other's arm, smiling and drawing close as they spoke. She swallowed down the familiar feeling of being on the outside. She had grown up a military brat, transforming herself to fit in at whatever new school she found herself in. Great training for an actor. Hard on her tender heart.

"Ciao!" she called. "Thanks for coming."

"Ciao!" a chorus called back, sounding exactly like her. She smiled. She liked that they felt comfortable enough to joke around with her now.

The door clicked shut behind them, the room

quiet and empty. Her smile dropped. She turned and headed for the private door in the back of the lounge, where her bodyguard, Frank, an enormous Hawaiian man with a shaved head and stone-faced expression, waited. She'd had to hire full-time security after *Neighborly Attraction* came out last year. She'd played the virginal heroine, who takes her sexy neighbor up on his offer for lessons in seduction. Too many fans had tried to get close enough to teach her more sex lessons. She'd nearly had a heart attack when she'd discovered a strange man naked in her bed in her San Francisco home. Fortunately he'd stayed in the bed, trying to coax her to join him with lines from the movie, while she ran to the safety of her car and peeled out of there.

She went to her penthouse suite, her buzz from the tequila and being with her friends fading. Her huge silent shadow, Frank, followed close behind. There were no adjacent rooms. She had the entire top floor, with Frank in the room directly below hers nearest the stairs. After he did a quick check of her rooms, she told him goodnight and stepped inside the marbled foyer. She moved through the suite, making herself stop and appreciate the opulent accommodations, all done in shades of white and silver with royal blue accents— two bedrooms, each with a king-size bed and walk-in closet, a living room with a big-screen TV and modern geometric paintings, a dining room with seating for eight, a kitchenette, and the best, a private outdoor terrace with a spectacular view of the city.

She told herself to shake off the melancholy. Sure, fame had a price, but she had all of this. And a career she loved. She kicked off her pumps and padded in her bare feet to the master bathroom to get ready for bed. She made herself admire the oversized tub with jets, separate double shower stall, and the long marble counter, stopping when she caught her reflection in the mirror. She almost didn't recognize herself for a moment. Her shoulder-length hair was dyed dark brown for the movie, and it made her hazel eyes look more brown than green. But it was the haunted, fatigued expression on her drawn face that made her gut twist. She looked as unhappy as she felt. Something she could never, ever let show in public.

She turned her back on her reflection. She could never admit it to anyone.

It was damn lonely at the top.

Her cell vibrated and she pulled it from her jeans pocket. A text from Hailey with the address for the picnic date. She sighed. She had to put an end to this silliness.

Another text came through. Meet him Monday at three.

Hey, she hadn't agreed to that.

Hailey texted an emoticon blowing a kiss. Claire found herself smiling. She knew Hailey meant well.

She texted back a smiley face. It all felt so normal. Texting silly things with friends. Claire could do that.

Jenny Coleman could do that and more.

Did she dare risk it? The idea took hold, blooming in her mind, filling her with giddy anticipation. He was book club approved. He was Mad's brother. He always took out women as part of Hailey's business plan in a perfectly gentlemanly way. The circumstances couldn't have been more ideal. It was practically risk-free as Jenny. Even if he recognized her in disguise, she could trust him by association not to spill her secret. Probably.

She quickly texted Hailey that she'd be there, turned, and caught her flushed happy expression in the mirror. She would take a chance on being her old regular self. She just hoped she remembered how.

CHAPTER TWO

Jake Campbell was on top of the world. He was the founder and CEO of a global tech company, Dat Cloud, that pioneered sharing and storing of memory-hogging data—pictures, audio, video—with an ease and speed that hadn't been possible before his data-compression application. He'd worked his ass off to get to where he was today, the company could practically run itself now, and here he was at a rooftop party of some animation studio head, surrounded by the elite few who'd garnered an invitation, when it hit him how very alone he felt. He rubbed at the ache in his chest and gazed out at the view of San Francisco Bay, reminding himself to appreciate the rewards his hard work had given him.

Ever since the company went public, he had more money than he knew what to do with and that gave him options—travel, rubbing elbows with the rich and famous, building his dream house to his exact specifications. But money had some nasty side effects. People always wanted something, approaching with a hand out for donations, investments, or unwarranted child support. The child-support thing pissed him off. It started when he'd been named Silicon Valley's sexiest bachelor two years ago, a dubious honor given the population of mostly tech geeks. In any case, beautiful women threw themselves at him, but they were only after one thing. Not the good thing either. The pattern was predictable. At first they'd be clingy, hoping for a commitment. Not gonna happen. Not that he was afraid of commitment, he'd been in two long-term relationships pre-sexiest bachelor days, he'd just never met the woman who made him *want* to settle down. He must be missing that nesting gene. That made sense, actually. No one in his family was in a committed relationship, not even his parents. So, there you go. Basic DNA deficiency.

Unfortunately, his natural reluctance to commit just made women try harder. In the past year, he'd had three women file paternity suits in a blatant grab for his money. Two of them he hadn't even slept with. Ridiculous. And not great for his reputation either. The third woman he had slept with, though he was sure she must've tampered with the condom because he never had unprotected sex. He'd been ready to step up with child support—he'd never make a kid suffer for the sins of the mother—but the paternity test proved he wasn't the father.

He just couldn't trust anyone anymore.

He raked a hand through his dark brown hair. He almost missed those early days in the business, seven years ago, fresh out of the army and working hard on this idea he'd had to make information sharing easier around the world. Now life was a plateau, no challenge, same old stuff. He turned away from the view and back to the party, thinking he should just bail. He didn't even know half the people here, and he wasn't up to small talk. *Shit.* He caught Priscilla's approach, someone he'd slept with once and couldn't seem to shake, and made a quick sideways move toward his friend and second in command at Dat Cloud, Steve Nelson. He was sick of glamorous, superficial women like her. Priscilla changed course and followed him.

"I'm taking off," he told Steve.

"Already?" Steve looked around Jake's shoulder, smiling in appreciation at Priscilla. She was a former bikini model, as she liked to tell everyone she met. Steve spoke under his breath. "Don't let Priscilla scare you off. I'll take her off your hands."

Jake grinned. Steve was wealthy, thanks to Dat Cloud, but he was also short and round with a preference for Grateful Dead shirts and Birkenstocks with socks. Women weren't throwing themselves at Steve. Though they should because he was a helluva guy with a good heart. He spent every other weekend with his sister's kids ever since their dad had taken off.

Priscilla wrapped sharp manicured nails around Jake's bicep. "There you are," she purred. "Let's get out of here."

"You remember Steve?" Jake asked.

"Sure, we've met a few times," Steve said with a big smile.

Priscilla looked at Steve blankly before turning her attention back to Jake. "I miss you. Always so busy. All work and no play is no fun at all." She made a small pout with her jumbo Botoxed lips. He stifled a smart-ass remark. He missed regular girls like the kind he'd grown up with, natural beauties ready for fun. At least they had been when he was in high school. Damn, he was getting all nostalgic. He was thirty-two, it wasn't like they'd be home waiting for him after all these years.

He peeled Priscilla off his arm. "I'm heading out."

"He needs his beauty sleep," Steve told Priscilla with a wink. "How about we…"

She frowned and stalked off.

"Another time," Steve muttered.

"You don't want her," Jake said. "Trust me."

"I'm doing shots," Steve said, heading to where a

bar was set up complete with a thatched roof.

Jake inclined his head and left him to it. He headed home in his eco-friendly electric Tesla Model S to his modern concrete and glass house. When he got inside, he wandered around, feeling restless. The house was all one level, an open floor plan with black leather sofa and chairs, glass tables, and steel accents. A large patio led to a pool and hot tub. He'd had an architect and interior designer execute his idea of luxury living. But now when he looked around, it felt kind of sterile and cold. A wave of homesickness hit him. His house growing up, a modest three-bedroom colonial, had always felt alive, crowded with people. He hadn't seen his family—his dad, four brothers, sister, and a tight group of blood brothers—in way too long.

It was near midnight back home in Eastman, Connecticut. His identical twin, Josh, would just be getting off work as a bartender with pockets full of tips from the ladies. His twin was the Sexiest Bachelor in Eastman—self-appointed—in response to Jake's sexiest bachelor title. As Josh put it, what woman could resist the allure of thick dark brown hair, deep brown bedroom eyes, wickedly sexy stubble, charming smile, and muscular athletic bod? Idiot.

Jake smiled to himself and pulled out his cell to text Josh only to find a text waiting for him. Spooky how "twin sense" could work on opposite sides of the country.

Josh: *Twin sense tells me u need a place 2 crash.*

Jake grinned. Whether it was twin sense or Josh was inviting him for a visit, it didn't matter. He'd take the jet first thing in the morning. His thumbs flew over the keys.

Jake: *I'll be there tomorrow afternoon. Dibs on the bed.*

Josh: *FU. My place, my bed. Not running a hotel.*

Jake chuckled. Josh had a one-bedroom apartment. He could get a hotel, but he'd take the sofa just to hang with Josh. As kids, even in the chaos of their large extended family, they'd always made sure to have twin time, just the two of them. "Twin refuel" they'd called it. They'd even had an elaborate high-five, low-five routine that ended with a revving engine of twin fuel. Corny, but true. Hell, they'd shared a womb— the ultrasound showed them hugging each other— shared a room growing up, even gone into the army at the same time, though different units. Jake had come out of the military driven to work with global technology that could open access to online education and opportunities in poor areas (and also caught on very lucratively in places that could well afford it). Josh came out of the army shell-shocked with what he'd seen and been through as a paratrooper dropped from a plane into enemy territory, where hand-to-hand combat was often required. He'd had a long recovery, but was doing better now.

Jake: *Time for a twin refuel.*

Josh: *Not in my bed, freak. Bring that $$$$ scotch.* He wanted the rare Macallan scotch. Jake had some vintage bottles.

Still feeling nostalgic for things back home, he texted, *How's Mad?* His little sister, Madison, was the baby and the only girl. He and his brothers looked out for her. Josh, more than any of them, made sure she was okay, even bringing her on part-time as bartender where he worked in Clover Park while she went to community college. School had been at Josh's insistence because he was tired of worrying about her bartending in a seedy part of New York City. Mad must've been tired of it too because she went for Josh's plan, and Mad didn't do anything she didn't want to do.

Josh: *Mad's Mad.*

Jake: *Kicking ass and taking names.*

Josh: *Yup.*

Jake: *How's Dad?*

Josh: *2 tired for 20 questions. See u later.*

Jake sent a smiley face emoticon with sunglasses just to annoy his brother, who believed emoticons were for teenaged girls. Probably because Mad used to emoticon the hell out of them in some hieroglyphic way that Jake suspected was code and Josh suspected was for her own amusement. He headed to the bedroom and started packing, the empty ache in his chest easing for the first time all night.

~ ~ ~

Twenty-four hours later, Jake leaned an elbow on the dark cherry bar at Garner's Sports Bar & Grill, where Josh worked, and took a long swallow of beer. It was Saturday night and the place was filling up fast. His brother was jovial, working the bar and the customers, especially the ladies, with equal ease. Some of the women slid him a napkin with a phone number scribbled on it. Josh tucked those numbers behind the bar with a smile like they were something special, but Jake knew he'd toss them in the nightly cleanup. Not that Josh didn't like hooking up with the ladies. He'd gotten plenty of action, but lately he'd been slacking. Even Jake couldn't get the reason out of him.

"What was wrong with that one?" Jake asked, referring to the curvy brunette that had just left with some friends. She'd gifted Josh a hefty tip and her number while leaning forward to give him a peek down her low-cut shirt.

Josh just shook his head, a small smile playing over his lips. He moved on to the next customer.

Damn. Was Josh holding out for something

more…serious? Looking to settle down? Was that what was going on in twin Campbell land? If his twin was ready, that meant maybe he was too. Their lives often paralleled each other. Like when they'd both dropped out of the same college two years in, feeling restless and needing adventure. Josh thought college was a waste of time, nothing held his interest, and the minute he said so to Jake, he admitted he'd been feeling the same way. He was a self-taught computer guy and knew more than his professors. Jake came up with the idea to enlist in the army since their dad was a veteran. Josh said why the hell not and went along for the ride. Jake still felt guilty over the way Josh's life had taken a bad turn after the army. He tried to console himself with the fact that Josh was damn happy with his life now.

Were they done with the bachelor scene? The idea of either of them settling down was so far-fetched. But it nagged at him, hovering over his head like a damn fly.

A beautiful redheaded woman appeared at his side. Her hair was long, a light reddish blonde, her pale blue eyes fixed on his brother. She wore a dark green dress that hugged a perfect hourglass figure and black strappy heels. Designer stuff from head to toe if he knew women. And he did.

"Josh," she called, frantically waving him over.

Josh's head swiveled around, his brown eyes narrowed, before he lifted a finger at her to wait and moved to the next customer.

The woman huffed and muttered, "Ignoring me. Cad."

She looked high maintenance. Perfect hair, perfectly made up, strikingly beautiful, but…

She turned to him and did a double take. "Oh my God! There's two of you!" She called to Josh, who was pouring some beer on tap. "You never told me you had a twin!"

"I haven't told you a lot of things," Josh returned.

The woman held out her hand with a polite smile, and Jake shook it. "I'm Hailey."

"Jake."

Josh appeared in front of them. "What can I get ya?"

"Do you still have Mondays off?" Hailey asked Josh.

"Yeah."

Hailey gestured Josh closer.

He rolled his eyes, but leaned across the bar. "What?"

She whispered, but Jake was still close enough to hear her ask, "Can you do a Monday date with a new member of the book club?"

Jake's gaze cut to Josh, who didn't seem at all fazed

by this odd question. Instead he stood straighter and looked vastly entertained. Since when did Josh do blind dates? He met women all the time at the bar. Not to mention all the women at the cooking classes he took because he claimed his boss at Garner's wanted him to, but Jake knew it was because Josh was a foodie and dreamed of opening his own bar with awesome food one day. If he'd let him, Jake would pony up the money in a heartbeat.

Hailey put a hand on her hip. "Well?"

Josh jerked his chin. "What's it worth to ya?" He grinned at Jake.

"The standard arrangement," Hailey said through clenched teeth. Jake got the feeling this was a frequent conversation.

Josh busied himself behind the bar, biting back a smile. Clearly he enjoyed messing with Hailey, who rose to the bait beautifully.

Her blue eyes flashed with annoyance. "So can you do it?"

"Hmm…" Josh said, jerking her chain some more.

Hailey turned to Jake unexpectedly. "Maybe you'd like to go on the date? Very sweet girl."

Jake opened his mouth to say he wouldn't be in town on Monday when Josh cut him off.

"He's on a hiatus from women." Josh smirked. "Billionaires have that falling-at-their-feet problem."

Jake glared at Josh. First of all, he'd never said he was on a hiatus, and second, he didn't appreciate the billionaire dig. Josh had a chip on his shoulder about being the non-billionaire twin. His brother was just as smart and could've gotten in on the ground floor of Dat Cloud, but he'd chosen a different less lucrative path. Besides, Jake had fallen out of the ten-figure club recently with an expansion into a country where the government was overturned by a dictator who seized all assets. A temporary dip, he was sure. He took big risks and was frequently rewarded with big gains. Or losses. Money was never a sure thing.

Hailey looked at Jake with new appreciation. "What do you do?"

"I started Dat Cloud. It's—"

"I read about Dat Cloud in the *Wall Street Journal!* We should talk. What are you doing tomorrow?"

He caught Josh's frown and realized his brother might actually want her for himself. Though he had a helluva weird way of showing it.

"Busy," Jake said.

"Can I buy you a drink?" Hailey asked, surprising him.

It had been a damn long time since someone bought *him* something.

"Sure," Jake said.

"Great!" Hailey exclaimed. "Josh, get him

whatever he'd like. On me."

"Another beer, barkeep," Jake ordered, tapping the bar.

Josh didn't move. "I'll take you up on that date, princess."

Hailey scowled. "Stop calling me that," she snapped.

"If the diamond tiara fits…" Josh drawled.

Hailey pasted on a smile and smoothed her dress. "I'll text you the details." She turned to Jake. "It was really nice to meet you." She whipped a card out of her purse and handed it to him. "Call me next time you're in town for a longer visit."

Josh shot him a dark look that he didn't need any twin sense to know meant Jake wasn't supposed to go there.

"Nice to meet you too," Jake said.

Hailey beamed a smile that made her incandescent. Her blue eyes lit like twin sparklers, her pale skin glowed pink, even her teeth seemed extra shiny white. He was momentarily held in thrall at her stunning beauty.

"Ciao!" She turned on her heel and strode out the door. She seemed to have forgotten she'd bought him a drink.

"Ciao," Jake said.

"Ciao," Josh muttered, his lip curling.

Jake turned to watch her go, unable to take his eyes off her curvy ass. A hard jab hit him between the shoulder blades. "Ow!"

He whirled, about to return the hit to his scowling brother, when Josh stepped out of reach and moved across the bar to help a customer.

Jake read the card Hailey had given him, puzzling over what a Love Junkie did. Was that part of her "arrangement" with Josh?

"So what's the arrangement?" Jake asked once Josh finally moved back to his side of the bar.

Josh didn't bother replying. Just straightened up, tucking used glasses away.

The next logical thought hit him with a jolt. He leaned across the bar and lowered his voice, "Are you a...male hooker?"

Josh moved to the other side of the bar without a word. Fuck. He couldn't believe it. Was he that hard up for funds for his dream bar?

Jake tried to get the details several more times, but Josh kept his mouth shut. Jake finally gave up and contented himself with watching the Sox game. But his curiosity over the strange interaction between Josh and Hailey got the better of him. He had to know what the deal was. He waited until Josh closed the bar and headed to the back parking lot to bring it up again. In a roundabout way.

"Why do you call Hailey a princess?" Jake asked.

"Why do you care?" Josh said with no real heat. He slid into his black Miata convertible.

Jake got in the passenger seat. "She's pretty. I might give her a call next time I'm in town."

Josh started the car and muttered under his breath, "Ass." He peeled out of the lot.

"So you don't like her, or you do? I can't tell."

"Drop it."

This Hailey thing just got more and more interesting. And troubling. Why was Josh being so close-lipped about it? What had he gotten himself into?

"Is she an actual princess?" Jake asked once they'd parked at the large Victorian house across town, where Josh rented the first-floor apartment.

Josh got out of the car and slammed the door. Jake kept up with him, their strides equally long-legged. "You messing with royalty?"

Josh shook his head and unlocked the door of the house and then the door to his apartment. He tossed his keys in a bowl by the front door and crossed to the long beige sofa with a chaise lounge on one end. Josh flopped on the sofa, stretching across the length of it. Jake took the chaise lounge and shoved his brother's feet away so he could stretch out too.

"You'd better not be doing anything illegal," Jake

said.

"Shut up already. Geez, you're worse than Mad with all your questions."

"Just tell me if you're a hooker," Jake said, half-joking. Really, it was an absurd thought. Neither of them had ever had any trouble getting a woman. "That's all I need to know before I go to the authorities."

Josh snorted. Their dad was a retired cop. "I'm not a hooker. More like a paid gentleman escort. No sex."

Jake jackknifed up and stared at his brother. "You're kidding, right?" Except Josh looked dead serious.

Josh closed his eyes. "I just do it to mess with her."

Jake was thoroughly confused. "You take women out for money to mess with a princess?" And no sex? What was the point in that?

Josh opened his eyes. "She's not a princess. Think about it. Why would a princess be hanging around a bar in the burbs, talking to me?"

"You tell me."

"I just call her that because she's like a princess." He tilted his nose up. "Above the riffraff."

"Because she's beautiful?" Jake guessed.

Josh threw an arm over his eyes. "It's her fancy designer dresses and her attitude."

Jake hadn't noticed an attitude. She'd seemed okay

to him. Whatever. If Josh wanted to mess with her and she kept rising to the bait, maybe that was just their idea of a good time. Though he couldn't remember his brother acting so strange before. Usually he was outrageously charming with women, and then once they did the deed, he lost interest. He had to wonder how long they'd been playing this game.

"You want some of that scotch?" Jake asked.

Josh lowered his arm. "You have to ask?"

He headed to the kitchen, where he'd left it, and poured them both a couple of tumblers. He returned to the sofa, where Josh was now sitting up, smiling at his cell phone.

"What?" Jake asked.

Josh shoved his phone in his pocket. "She just texted me that she'd like to skip the cash for this date and give me brownies instead."

"You'll go through the hassle of a blind date for brownies?"

"They're really good. They're fudgy and perfectly—" he kissed his fingers "—luscious. I've only had them once and I'm trying to figure out the secret ingredient."

Jake stared at him.

Josh gestured for the glass. "Drink?"

Jake handed it over. They clinked glasses before downing the whole thing in one long swallow in perfect unison. One of those twin things.

"How much does she normally pay you?" Jake asked, pouring more scotch into Josh's outstretched tumbler and then into his own.

Josh lifted his glass in a silent thank you and tossed it back. "I'll pay her back one day."

Jake shook his head at the cagey answer. "How long have you been doing this?"

Josh lifted one shoulder up and down. "Three months."

Jake sipped his scotch. They really should savor ten-thousand-dollar scotch. "How in the world did you come up with this scam?"

Josh lifted a palm. "She's ambitious. She wants to build her wedding planning business and needs a regular date to weddings. We met at a cooking class, and she asked me out in a professional capacity. Her words. She figured out I'm more reliable than the twentysomething dudes she's used to." His lips twitched on "dudes," and he hid a smile with another sip of scotch.

"For a price. Or brownies." Jake puzzled over this strange arrangement. "Wait, so how did wedding dates with her lead to you going on blind dates with someone else?"

"Yeah. Well…" He helped himself to more scotch.

"Slow down," Jake said. "That's the good stuff."

Josh sipped. "It is good."

"So? What's the deal with the blind dates?"

Josh swirled his scotch before tossing back half the glass. He coughed. "She, uh, wants me to warm up the women before she gets them back out in the dating world. First step on her wedding planning journey. She's got a business plan and everything." He smiled to himself at that. "Anyway, the women have usually been burned before and need a guy like me."

"A paid escort kind of guy?" Jake was having trouble wrapping his head around what the hell his twin was doing and why.

Josh narrowed his eyes. "A guy who shows them not all men are slime. I give them the gentleman treatment and tell them right up front I'm not looking for serious, just one fun date." He shrugged. "It goes fine. No hard feelings."

Their dad had drummed acting like a gentleman into all of their thick skulls. He could hear him now. "You treat a lady *right*. That means manners, holding doors, speaking respectfully." His dad's mom had been mistreated and his dad's stepdad had made a world of difference with much more respectful gentlemanly ways. Unfortunately, that gentleman thing hadn't panned out for their dad. His beauty queen wife, their mom, hadn't stuck around despite being treated like a queen. She'd left her husband and six kids without a backward glance. Mad, the youngest, had only been one.

Jake studied his twin, still not sure what Josh was getting out of this deal. Some cash? Brownies? It sounded like a whole lot of effort for not much in return. "I don't get it."

"It's a transaction," Josh said like Jake was a moron. "She's the one that keeps coming back for more."

"You do like her!"

Josh stood, finished his drink, and set the glass on the coffee table. "I'm beat." He stretched and did a big fake yawn.

Jake socked him in the gut. Josh returned the punch, knocking the scotch bottle, but Jake snagged it, managing not to spill any.

"Fine," Jake said. "Go to bed, wuss."

Josh laughed. "Night." He headed toward his bedroom with his usual laid-back amble.

"Why don't you ask her out?" Jake called.

Josh stopped and spoke without turning around. "She's got higher ambitions than a bartender."

"How do you know?"

Josh turned, his eyes hooded and tired. "You saw the way she warmed up to you once she heard you had money."

Jake slowly shook his head. "No. She didn't ask me

out. She just said we should talk."

"She bought you a drink."

"Not really. She left without paying for it."

Josh's jaw went tight. "Believe me, she's into the money thing."

Jake leaned his head back on the sofa. "I'm so tired of women only looking for one thing."

"Must be rough."

"You know what I mean."

A slow smile dawned on Josh's face. "You want to teach Hailey a lesson?"

The hair on the back of his neck stood up. His body suddenly felt charged and alert. "Man, we haven't done the switcheroo in ages."

Josh's eyes gleamed. "You go on the sweet-girl-from-book-club date; I'll go out with Hailey as you and show her she really does like slumming with me."

Jake frowned. If Josh actually did like Hailey, this seemed like a shitty thing to do to her. On the other hand, maybe if Josh went out with Hailey on a real date, it would end this weird brownie/cash dance they were doing.

"I'll tell her at the end of the date who I really am," Josh said, answering his unspoken objection. "I just want to, you know, open her ambitious eyes."

And yours. "She's gonna be pissed."

"I'll deal with Hailey. And your girl won't care.

You're just the warm-up to dating again. Can you stay until Tuesday?" Josh suddenly looked more awake. "We'll do the date on Monday at the same time so they don't have a chance to talk to each other about it."

Jake considered his role in this. He'd never had a blind date.

"Come on. You know you love it."

He did. It was freeing to be someone else. And it had always been easy to step in for his twin. They knew each other as well as they knew themselves. And it might be cool to see how the other half lived. What his life would've been like if he'd stayed back east and had hometown roots like Josh did. A casual no-stress lifestyle sounded fantastic. A sweet small-town girl too, like the kind he'd grown up with.

"I'm in," Jake said.

They grinned at each other. "Awesome," they said in unison.

"Who gets the brownies?" Jake asked.

"Me."

"Hey," Jake protested. "Why do I get the blind date, no cash, and no brownies?"

"World history."

"Come on. That was high school." Josh had taken Jake's place for a world history final exam senior year because Jake had stayed up all night playing poker in a friend's basement. Fortunately, they'd been in two different classes, so the switcheroo worked.

"You graduated, didn't you?"

"What about Sherri Wexton? I took her out while you were busy with Tanya what's-her-name."

Josh smiled in memory; then he countered with, "Missy Pardo."

"Bah." They could do this all night with all the trading places they used to do, usually involving keeping a bunch of girls interested and not pissing any of them off. Not one girl had ever noticed which twin they were with. Most people couldn't tell them apart. Except family and the rare few who really got to know them.

"Fine." Jake put a hand over his heart. "I'll do it out of the goodness of my heart. Only because you're so twisted up over Hailey."

"I'm not twisted."

Jake raised his brows.

"Shut up," Josh said and headed to bed.

CHAPTER THREE

Jake waited in the gravel parking lot by the Saugatuck River in Greenport for his redheaded mystery date in Josh's black board shorts, white tee, and beat-up rubber sandals. Josh would be wearing Jake's custom Italian suit. He'd left a few suits at his dad's house in case of some celebratory occasion. He'd given his twin a wad of cash to take Hailey out to a top Michelin-rated restaurant in the city and arranged for a private room in a nearby bar if they wanted to extend the evening. He suspected Josh would. Of course, that depended on Hailey being cool about the switcheroo when Josh did the big *ta-da* reveal at the end of dinner. He kinda wished he could be there for that. For himself, his true identity didn't matter. It was a onetime thing.

No one else was here, except for the old guy sitting in the nearby boating rental shed. At least it was one of those Indian summer days, eighty degrees. Perfect.

Jake figured they could do some paddleboarding before their hike and picnic. The trails were right across the street. He loved paddleboarding, and the river was nice and calm, even a beginner could handle it. His gaze caught on the approach of a woman, her head ducked shyly, her face in shadow, with a tan baseball cap pulled down low and large round sunglasses. She had straight red hair that ended just past her jaw. It must be her.

He strode toward her, quickly remembered he was Josh, and slowed it down to a laid-back amble. Besides the cap, she was all in black—black tank top, black shorts, black flip-flops. The hot rush of lust caught him by surprise. Her tank was modest, but her breasts were full, her waist narrow, her hips a sweet curve down to trim, toned legs. His gaze took the return trip back up to her face, which he still couldn't get a good look at. Nothing about her said *look at me,* yet he couldn't look away. He found the modest shyness appealing. This woman was as far from the glamorous superficial women he'd dated as you could get.

He stopped in front of her, mindful to keep a respectful distance like the gentleman he never was. She was petite, her head level with his chest. He smiled. "Hi, I'm Josh."

She didn't respond at first. He peered under her cap, trying to get a look at her face, mostly covered by the pulled-down brim and large sunglasses. Her skin was creamy and flawless, her lips full and luscious. Not a drop of makeup. A natural beauty.

He offered his hand. "You must be Jenny."

Instead of shaking hands, she slowly took off her sunglasses, her bright green eyes meeting his directly. A jolt ran through him. Their gazes locked and a bone-deep recognition of *something* about her spoke to him. Like he was meant to meet her. Like some part of him already knew her. The blood surged through his veins. Like fate.

Damn, he didn't even believe in fate, but he didn't know how else to explain the rightness of the connection.

He shook his head. "Sorry for staring. Your eyes are such a bright green."

She laughed, a throaty, husky sound that grabbed him by the balls. "I had to get a good look at you too. You've got the book club stamp of approval." She flashed a stunningly white smile. "I had to make sure that was a good thing."

Her throaty sexy voice immediately made him think of things he had no business thinking about. He was supposed to be taking a sweet girl out as the charming gentleman bartender. Building his own company from the ground up had taught him that it paid to be an aggressive go-getter. A natural spillover into his personal life hadn't steered him wrong. He got what he wanted, for the most part, because he went after it. He told himself to dial it back. He was Josh today, and Jenny couldn't help the way she sounded. Maybe she was a smoker. Though she didn't smell like cigarettes. She smelled sweet like vanilla and sugar. Probably some kind of body wash. But, hell, it worked. He could breathe her in all day. And night.

He offered his arm, crooking it at the elbow, like a total gentleman. "Shall we?"

She slid her shades back on. "Just a minute." She pulled her cell from her shorts pocket and sent a quick text.

He'd left his cell phone and wallet in the car, not wanting them to get wet. Besides, he'd wanted to unplug today.

"Okay." She tucked her phone away and took his arm, her hand resting lightly on his forearm, warming him on the spot. Her nails were polish-free. He didn't know why he found that so appealing, he just knew that he did. She felt real.

He turned to her. "You might want to put your cell in your car."

"That's okay. I was dropped off."

"I can put it in my car. You don't want it to get wet."

She stiffened. "Wet?"

"I thought we'd go paddleboarding before our picnic." He gestured over to the river. "It's nice and calm. Have you paddleboarded before?"

She let go of his arm and pulled her cap down even further, securing it all around the edges. "No."

He peeked under her cap. "It's an hour rental. A three-and-a-half-mile route under the bridge and out to some small islands. There's supposed to be a fantastic view of the Long Island Sound."

She looked down at herself. "I'm not wearing a swimsuit."

"I'll make sure you don't get wet. I'll help you on and off the board. It's really stable." He elbowed her gently. "Come on. It'll be fun."

She rocked on her heels. He sensed she was leaning toward trying it, so he made her an offer she couldn't refuse. "If you get even one drop of water on you, I'll let you call me foxy for the rest of the day."

She laughed. "Oh, you will? What an honor!"

"I know, right? Just trust me. I wouldn't steer you wrong."

"I don't even know you. How can I trust you?" It wasn't a no. And she was smiling.

He raised his palms. "I'm book-club approved. How many guys can say that?"

"You're the only one I've heard of."

"There you go." He gestured for her phone. "I'll

put it in my car for you."

She looked at him for a long moment. He wiggled his fingers. She bit back a smile, powered down the phone, and handed it over.

"Be right back." He jogged over to his rental car and stashed it with his. He returned to her side and offered his arm.

"Such a gentleman," she said in a teasing voice, but he could tell she liked it. She rested her hand lightly on his arm.

They crossed to the shed marked Boating Rentals, where a guy with thinning white hair sat, watching a boxing match on a small TV.

"Two paddleboards, please," Jake said.

She let go of his arm and walked near the water's edge. He pulled the cash from his pocket and paid the guy, who could barely tear his gaze away from the TV, even as he handed over two life vests and directed them to the launch place.

Jake called over to Jenny and gestured for her to follow. Her stride was confident, comfortable in her own skin, and extremely sensual, graceful with a nice breast bounce. He reminded himself he was a gentleman today and focused on her unpainted toes. Even those looked good enough to suck. Geez. He felt like a perv. He didn't have a toe fetish and, after his previous nightmare dealings with gold-digging women these past two years, he was much slower to warm up to someone new. But there was something different about Jenny. He'd passed warmed-up and went straight to blazing lust just standing next to her. If they ever got skin on skin—

A gentleman wouldn't do that. Josh wouldn't do that.

Jake would.

Damn, this switcheroo date just got a lot more complicated.

Her sexy toes reached him, and he lifted his head to meet her eyes. He saw only his reflection in her large shades. He wished he could see those green eyes again. They were amazing.

"I take it this one is mine?" she asked in her husky phone-sex operator voice. She took the smaller life vest from his hand while he was still lost in lust land. "Of course I won't be needing it, seeing as how you promised I wouldn't get wet."

"That's right. Just a legal safety requirement." He put on his life vest. "Have you ever done a blind date before?"

Her lips played at a smile. "No."

He headed toward the paddleboards. "What made you agree to go?"

"Oh, you know." She waved a hand in the air. "Same old story. Burnt by love, slowly making my way back to the dating scene. And you know Hailey."

He scrambled for an appropriate response because he didn't know Hailey. "She's a piece of work," he said just like Josh would. "But she means well."

A moment passed where he feared he'd screwed up because Jenny was just staring at him, but then she said, "Exactly. Plus you're Mad's brother, so you must be okay. She cracks me up."

He started at the mention of his sister and quickly covered by grabbing a couple of paddles. She knew Mad? His sister didn't have women friends. She'd always been one of the guys. "Mad Campbell?" he asked just to be sure.

She studied him. "You are Josh Campbell?"

"Yeah, yeah. Mad's in your book club?"

"She didn't tell you?"

He shook his head.

She laughed, that throaty, husky sound that made him want to do dirty, dirty things. "Probably embarrassed to admit to her brother she's in a romance book club."

"Romance?" he asked incredulously. "Mad Campbell?"

She grinned. "I'm sensing some brotherly payback."

He handed her a paddle. "Oh yeah."

"My turn. Why did you go on this blind date? I

heard you do these regularly."

He lifted one shoulder up and down. "Chance to take out a sweet girl. Treat her right and show her not all men are slime." He figured that sounded very gentlemanly and Josh had said that. Though Josh's real reasons screamed Mr. Ulterior Motive.

She tilted her head. "Seriously? That's all you got?"

He scrambled for an even more Josh-like answer. "I treat women the way I'd want my sister to be treated. It's kinda my thing." This was actually true. Josh was weird like that. He'd taken on a *put out into the world what you want to see* philosophy when he'd gotten out of the army. Obviously there was zero correlation between the way he treated his dates and the way some Joe Shmoe treated their sister. Jake treated women well, but he put zero thought into the little sister angle. Besides, Mad could hold her own. She was a black belt and skilled with weapons. Honestly, she scared most men away with her don't-mess-with-me attitude.

"That's nice," Jenny said softly. "A protective older brother thing. I get that. I have an older brother too."

"He good to you?"

"Yeah. He's a good big brother."

"That's the best kind. I'm the oldest and I'm sure my siblings would agree I'm awesome." He grinned, and she laughed. He'd beat Josh out of the womb by two minutes. He kicked off his sandals. "The guy said we could leave our shoes here. No one will take them." She slipped out of her flip-flops, and he tucked their shoes behind the paddleboard stand.

He grabbed a bright blue paddleboard. "Lucky for you, I'm an expert paddleboarder."

"That is lucky," she said with a throaty chuckle. He could listen to that sexy voice all day long. But it wasn't just about her effortless sexiness, he felt so comfortable with her, like he knew her already. There was something vaguely familiar about her, though they'd never met. He didn't know what it was, he only knew he wanted to soak her up as much as he could on the one date allotted him.

Maybe he'd negotiate for more than one date. Everything was negotiable.

He watched as she took a smaller yellow paddleboard for herself. He was ready to step in and help with the weight of the board, but she handled it easily, surprisingly strong for her size. She looked about Mad's height, five three maybe to his six foot.

"Next step," he said, heading to the water. He walked in up to his calves and suppressed a wince at the chill of the water. He set the board down. "Start with the board in the water. Then get on the board on your knees. Strap the leash to your ankle once you're on so the board doesn't slip away from you. Then paddle out, pushing off on either side of the board. When you're ready, slowly stand, shoulder-width apart, in the center of the board. Feet parallel to each other. Don't go surfer on me." He did a surfer impression, one foot in front of the other. He suddenly realized she couldn't see his feet in the water. "That probably would've worked better on shore. I have one foot in front of the other."

She laughed. "I got it. But, foxy, you're going to help me on this board or it ain't happening."

"Foxy, I like it. We'll have to come up with a new name for you to call me if you get wet."

"I could think of a few more colorful words for that scenario."

"I bet." He waded back out to her, setting his board on shore. He took her board and set it in the water. "On your knees."

Her jaw dropped comically.

He laughed. "I just realized how that sounded. I just meant…it's easier to balance if you start on your knees. Bring your paddle too."

She grinned and stepped into the river with the paddle. "Ah! It's freezing!"

"Come on. It's not that bad."

"It's bad!" She did a little dance and turned to go back on shore.

He snagged her by the elbow and pulled her next

to the board. "I'll strap your ankle to the board as soon as you get on."

She stared at the board.

"Look, I got it." He had both hands on the board, holding it steady.

She jabbed a warning finger in his face that had him grinning. Then she flashed a brief smile and got on the board, kneeling. He quickly strapped her ankle in place.

"You can swim, right?" he asked with a straight face.

She glared at him; even through her shades he could feel it. "I will throttle you with my bare hands if I take a dive in this river."

He chuckled. "Bloodthirsty. All right, now stand and get your balance. I'll keep it steady while you push off with the paddle."

"Feels like training wheels." She slowly stood, feet shoulder-width apart as he'd instructed. After a moment, she announced, "Okay, about to paddle."

He held on lightly as she pushed off in one smooth stroke, and then he let go. She had good balance.

"Woo! I did it!" she exclaimed.

"More like *I* did it."

"Shut up, foxy! Hurry up and catch up. I don't know how to stop this thing."

He got on his board and pushed off, quickly

catching up to her.

She beamed, her teeth sparkling white in the sunshine. "This is fun! I have no idea how to turn, but a straight line seems to be working okay."

"Keep your knees bent a little. When you want to turn, put the paddle on the opposite side of the turn and twist your body toward the side you want to turn."

"I'll watch you."

"And move your hands further apart. One on the handle, one on the shaft."

She adjusted her hands.

"You're a natural," he said, impressed. The first time he'd gone paddleboarding, he'd fallen in three times before getting his footing. Of course, she had him to do the difficult part of getting up on the board. He'd only had his friend Steve laughing his ass off at him.

"Must be all those Pilates," she said.

All the women he met out in California were fanatical about Pilates and yoga. "You into all that Pilates yoga stuff?"

"Just a little routine I do at home."

Of course she probably couldn't afford a fancy gym membership. Actually he didn't even know what she did for a living, just that she was a small-town girl. "What do you do?"

"You mean my job?"

"Yeah."

"I'm a personal trainer," she said and pulled in front of him in one big power stroke. That explained her ease with the paddleboard.

He watched her paddle for a moment. "Make sure you put your back into the stroke, not your arms," he called. "Dip the paddle deep into the water and do one long stroke."

"Got it."

He caught up with her. They paddled for a few minutes, the only sound their paddles dipping into the water. The sun was shining, the birds were chirping, and the occasional car from the road by the dock was a distant soft hum. He took a deep breath in and out, relaxing.

He turned, caught her gaze, and they grinned at each other.

"I missed being out in nature like this," she said.

"Me too."

"I thought you did this all the time, Mr. Expert Paddleboarder."

"It's been a while." For more than just paddleboarding. As jaded as he'd become with women, she was like a breath of fresh air. He really liked her.

They paddled in companionable silence. The distant din of work and his constant to-do list fell away. No wonder Josh was one happy guy. This was the life. Casual dates with sweet what-you-see-is-what-you-get girls, no stress, no deadlines, just life on his terms. Damn, he could get used to this.

But this wasn't his life. And he wasn't so sure one date would be enough with Jenny. He paddled and told himself to focus on the beautiful scenery, but the thought lodged in his brain, how to make this time with Jenny more than a onetime thing. He quickly decided if things went as well as he hoped today, he'd jet home every weekend. She'd never have to know he wasn't local.

No. That wasn't the Josh way. Casual meant casual. One date just for fun.

He glanced over at her sexy body, lingering on the curve of her smooth shoulder. How did Josh do casual when he actually met someone he liked? Had he *ever* met someone he liked on one of these casual blind dates? His board suddenly wobbled as his paddle tangled with some plants. Damn. He wasn't paying attention. He tore his gaze away from her shoulder. That could've been bad. Soaked in the river over one sweet shoulder.

"You okay there, foxy?" she asked in a teasing voice.

"Just fine, thank you."

She laughed.

He had the strangest urge to say *I really like you, I want to see you again, I want to hear that throaty, husky voice all night long*, but he couldn't. Because he was Josh. He suddenly wanted to reveal who he really was. But Josh hadn't done his switcheroo date yet, that started at dinner tonight. And if Jenny got mad and told Hailey, which he was sure she would, women stuck together, they'd both be dumped. So he said the only thing he could say.

"Race you to the bridge."

He put his back into it, taking off with powerful strokes, and she did too. It was on.

Chapter Four

Claire was having a fabulous time paddling down the river. Jenny was initially a role, but as she relaxed with Josh, who was supremely sweet and considerate, she became more and more herself. And holy crap, he was hot. The man did not need to be doing blind dates at all. She met plenty of gorgeous men, and, while Josh wasn't chiseled perfection, he was extremely appealing. His thick dark brown hair curled a bit at the nape of his neck, making her itch to run her fingers through it. Add in sexy stubble along a square jaw and an athletic muscular build, and all she wanted to do was rub shamelessly against him. And she was not the kind to rush into anything physical. Not with her past experiences with men eager to kiss and tell. But it was so much more than his looks. Something that pulled at her in a magnetic attraction. Confidence? The sparkle of good humor in those deep brown eyes? Pheromones? He smelled fantastic when she'd gotten up close to him back on shore, like warm woodsy spice and man. The attraction was real, even if Jenny wasn't, like a living breathing thing between them.

He hadn't recognized her, which was a little shocking, honestly. Even with the red-haired wig and green contacts, she thought he would. She'd been planning to swear him to secrecy or sic Mad on him, but…nothing. Maybe he was one of those rare people who didn't see her movies. Her biggest hits were chick flicks. Maybe he was a car chase movie kind of guy. But did he never see her splashed on magazine covers, the Internet, or supermarket tabloids? How could he *not* recognize her? It was a little disconcerting. She would certainly recognize a famous face even with different coloring. Did she look that un-glam without makeup? She almost wanted to ask him if she looked familiar, but that would just be her ego needing a pat. She kept paddling, sneaking looks at his muscular arms flexing as he paddled. With the jumbo shades she wore, he couldn't tell she was checking him out.

He must be doing this blind-date thing for some ulterior motive because there was no way he wasn't meeting plenty of willing women at the bar where he worked. He probably went on these casual dates to tweak Hailey's nose, but at the moment, Claire didn't care. This worked perfectly for her. Just one date. One glorious day to drop all the trappings of her life and just relax.

They were paddling back to shore now. She'd picked up paddleboarding quickly. It was a core workout, something she regularly worked on with her personal trainer. Thank goodness. The last thing she needed was to take a dive in the water and have her wig come off. She had all sorts of disguises for those times when she needed to get in and out of a place without a big crush of people. She preferred not to hide, but sometimes she had to.

So far, they'd hardly run into anyone on the river. Just a couple of fellow paddleboarders. She actually relaxed. No one wanted a piece of Jenny. She could move about freely. She hadn't realized how much she'd missed that simple joy.

Josh got to shore first. He waded back into the water and helped her off her paddleboard as promised, unstrapping her ankle from the board leash and then lifting her by the waist and setting her on shore. His hands didn't linger, merely assisted her in a gallant gesture. Total gentleman, as Hailey had promised.

"Thank you," she said.

He flashed a smile that made her pulse thrum. "No problem. I'll return these, grab our shoes, and then we'll get the picnic dinner Hailey packed for us."

"Hailey packed it? Oh, that is so sweet. Where is it?" She'd thought it would just be takeout from a deli or something.

"It's in a cooler in my car. I'll grab it and then we'll hit the hiking trails. Just over that way." He gestured across the road to the woods.

Here I go into the woods with a strange man. Alone. Vulnerable. Free.

"Can I get my cell?" she asked. She wanted to thank Hailey for the picnic.

He set one board down, pulled a remote key fob from his pocket, and aimed it at his white BMW, unlocking it. She headed for the car. There was something about him, something innately good that made her trust him. She'd spent a lifetime studying people, observing their mannerisms, gestures, expressions and how that either worked with or contradicted what they said. It was part of what made her a good actress. Josh just seemed authentic. A salt-of-the-earth bartender who looked out for his little sister. And book-club approved. You really couldn't get any better than that.

She snagged her cell from the glove compartment and powered it on, watching Josh's wide shoulders and back as he hauled the paddleboards to the stand. She glanced at her cell, punched in the code, and saw a text from Hailey. *How's it going?*

Great! Thanks for the picnic.

Did you like the cake?

There was cake? She did a quick battle with herself over the calories and quickly decided the workout today warranted it. *We didn't eat yet. Just finished paddleboarding.*

You paddleboarded? Cool! Do you like him?

She smiled. *He's awesome.*

Yay! I gotta run. A big opportunity came up.

Big wedding?

No. More later. Have fun!

She tucked the phone away just as Josh was heading toward her, carrying her flip-flops. He set them near her feet.

"How you feel?" he asked. "Sore?"

She slipped her shoes on. "Nope. I feel great."

"Awesome." He retrieved his wallet and cell from the glove compartment and tucked them into his pockets. Then he hit another button to pop the trunk.

She followed him to the trunk, where he hauled out the cooler.

"Grab the blanket," he said.

There was a green and white striped blanket rolled up with a strap. A picnic blanket. How cute! She grabbed it, tucking the strap over her shoulder, when it occurred to her a bartender probably couldn't afford a BMW. He shut the trunk and locked the car remotely.

"Nice car," she said.

He stared at the car for a moment and then turned

to her with a sheepish grin. "Rental."

"I thought you were from here."

"My car's in the shop."

"So you rented a really expensive car?"

He lifted one shoulder up and down. "I wanted to see how the other half lived."

An uneasy feeling went through her. Something wasn't adding up. "Why?"

He grinned. "Why not? Come on." He led the way through the gravel parking lot and across the road to the woods.

She kept up, wondering if she'd misjudged him. Had the pheromones distracted her? Was he not what he seemed? Something felt off. They stopped at a small wooden sign pointing the way to beginner, intermediate, and advanced hiking routes.

"What do you think?" Josh asked.

"Beginner," she said, figuring she could find her way back quickly if she needed a fast escape.

He blew out a breath and wiped his brow in an exaggerated gesture of relief. "I was hoping you'd pick that one. I'm not much of a hiker and I'd hate for us to get lost on our first date."

She studied him. "Do you think there will be a second date?" Some part of her wanted more than one date with Josh even though she knew it was impossible. She could only play at a normal life. And she needed to be sure he understood so no one got hurt.

He flashed a charming smile, his brown eyes sparkling with humor. "I guess you'll let me know after the first date."

"I thought you weren't looking for serious."

He stopped smiling. "I'm getting the feeling you don't want a second date."

"It's just that I'm really busy at work and not looking for a relationship."

"Ah." He looked away.

Shit. She hadn't meant to…did she hurt his feelings? "I'm sorry—"

"Hey, I know the deal." He met her eyes again, all traces of humor gone. "One date."

Now why did she have that awful ache of loneliness again? Like they were already saying goodbye. She forced herself to stay in the moment. "Yes. One *fun* date. I'm having a really good time."

"Good," he said. "Me too."

She reached over and snagged his free hand. He gave her a slow, sexy smile that sent warmth all the way through her, down to her toes.

They started down the beginner's path together. The dirt-packed trail was wide enough to fit three people across. She had to admit it was relaxing to be with a gentleman. Most guys were aggressive with her, wanting something, either a favor for their career or something physical. She hadn't felt this comfortable with a man since she'd catapulted into the spotlight.

"So tell me what keeps you so busy at work?" he asked.

She had her story ready. "I just went out on my own and I'm working to build my client base. Half my time is working with clients, half marketing." She knew a lot about personal trainers given her close friendship with her own personal trainer, Marsha. Of course, Marsha was paid big bucks to talk to her while she pushed Claire to stay in top condition. Most people she talked to were in her employment.

"Sounds ambitious," he said.

"I can be. But then I realized I needed to get off the hamster wheel and just let loose."

He grinned. "I'm with you on that. It seems we met at a perfect time for both of us to let loose."

"What do you do for fun?"

"Hang with the boys. Flirt with the pretty girls."

She caught his playful leering grin and shook her head with a smile. "Who are the boys?"

"My brothers and the blood brothers I grew up with."

"Blood brothers as in you did one of these?" She let go of his hand and mimed slicing her finger and pressing her two fingers together.

"More like we beat the crap out of each other until we knew who stood where in the pack. Lot of bloody noses."

"Like dogs."

"Pups. We were pups." He snagged her hand again. "My dad's a cop and he put us in the Police Athletic League, where his friend coached, because the five of us Campbell boys were acting out. We went a little nuts because…well, for a good reason. Anyway, we were quickly toe-to-toe with some kids who were acting out on a whole 'nother level. I mean really bad. They called themselves the Lost Boys, but after much fighting, the Campbells joined forces with them." He shook his head, smiling in memory. "Our coach, Chief Bailey, made us change the name to the Found Boys because we found each other and that meant we'd never be lost again."

Her heart squeezed. "That's really nice. And you're all still close?"

"Yeah."

"How old were you when you first became friends?"

"Nine."

"And you're what now?"

"Thirty-two."

"That's unusual to have a close group of friends from that far back. How many are there?"

"Me, four brothers, plus Mad—she's one of the guys—and five blood brothers, so that's eleven. There used to be a sixth blood brother, so we all matched up, six Campbells, six Found Boys, but we lost one."

"You mean—"

"He died."

"Oh, I'm so sorry."

"Thanks," he said solemnly.

She stayed quiet, not wanting to disturb his moment of remembrance.

He went on. "He wasn't a Campbell, but damn, we wanted him in with us. Nick was reckless, a tough fighter, but also loyal. He died not long after he dropped out of high school, getting tangled up with some local drug kingpins. It drew the rest of us tighter together." He cleared his throat. "So, you know, a bunch of us stayed local. Still get together for Saturday basketball, regular cookouts. Some of them coach in the Police Athletic League to mentor the younger kids."

His words of a tight brotherhood weren't matching the feeling radiating off him, which was longing and sadness.

"You okay?" she asked.

"Yeah." He flashed a smile that didn't fool her for a minute, but she didn't know him well enough to pry.

"Hailey says there's cake," she informed him

brightly.

"Nice. I didn't even look in the cooler. What kind?"

"No idea."

"Hey, any kind is good. She sure knows how to make a good blind date."

She couldn't disagree. They turned deeper into the woods. Josh asked her questions about her family, and she didn't have to lie. Her background was humble enough, moving from army base to army base every two to three years around the world. Turned out his family had a history of army service too. His dad got out while Josh was still young, so he didn't move around a lot like she did. She and her older brother by four years, Rich, had to work hard to find their way in each new place. Her brother had sports. She had acting, though she left that part out. Her time spent trying to fit in as a kid was in many ways the key to her acting. Her mom had encouraged her, signing her up for acting classes whenever possible. She shared the part of her she could share, telling him of her love for books.

He smiled and nodded. "Figured you were into books since you're in a book club."

They reached the end of the trail a short while later and stood in a grassy clearing overlooking a bubbling brook. A couple of dark green metal picnic tables and a well-used grill caked with black charcoal stood to one side. The grill was kind of gross; hopefully they didn't need to cook anything. They had the place all to themselves. It seemed a Monday date was great for avoiding being seen. She'd have to remember that.

Josh headed for the picnic table with the most shade and set the cooler on top. She set the blanket on the bench, figuring they didn't need it with the table. She peeked in the cooler as Josh started unpacking it. Hailey had outdone herself. Two bottles of white wine, three kinds of cheese, grapes, a baguette, and a huge slice of chocolate cake. No cooking, thank goodness. There were also plates, plastic wineglasses, napkins, plastic forks and knives, a corkscrew, and some bottled waters. The woman had gone above and beyond and Claire couldn't thank her enough. What a thoughtful gesture.

She took out a couple of bottled waters and then the wine. "I didn't want to come at first, but I'm glad I did."

He smiled, making crinkles form at the corners of his eyes. She liked that, like he probably laughed a lot. "Me too," he said warmly.

Her heart thumped a little harder. She dipped her head shyly the way Jenny would, but mostly because she wanted to hide the flush she could feel on her cheeks. She felt almost buzzed, though they hadn't opened the wine, every nerve ending alert and tingling. Was it the freedom of moving around without the crush of people? Or was it the magic of a date with Josh?

She took a sip of water. Then she uncorked the chilled white wine and poured them both a glass. She sat at the table as Josh set all the food out and tucked the cooler away. He sat across from her and lifted his wineglass to hers.

"To Hailey," he said.

She clinked his glass and accidentally knocked it too hard, making it slosh over his hand. "Oops!"

"Don't worry about it," he said with a laugh. He sucked wine off his hand and she suddenly wished she was the one lapping it up.

"To Hailey," she said.

They drank.

She was starving after their workout and snagged a hunk of havarti cheese, taking a bite.

He held up his glass again.

Her mouth was full of cheese. She chewed quickly. "Another toast?"

"Yeah."

She grabbed her glass and held it up.

"To you, Jenny. Just the sweetness I needed today."

"Aww," she said around the cheese. She couldn't

afford to be sweet most days or people would take advantage. It was nice to play sweet Jenny. She chewed some more and swallowed. "Thank you. You're sweet too. I've never had the gentleman treatment before."

"Well, you should."

They clinked glasses and drank again. They were both hungry and made short work of the food, talking easily about their favorite TV shows. They both loved to binge watch *Lost*. She didn't ask about movies, not wanting him to suddenly put her face to her real name. Finally they made it to the slice of cake in a plastic cake container that preserved the icing perfectly. Josh took off the lid and she stared at it, her mouth watering. Five layers with decadent chocolate ganache on top, chocolate icing between each layer.

Josh caught her eying the cake. "You can have it."

"Oh no. We can share. There's plenty for both of us."

"You look like you want to inhale it."

She grinned. "Personal trainers don't eat much sugar." Or actresses.

"We'll do the intermediate trail after this to work it off." He speared a forkful and offered it to her. She took it and closed her eyes, savoring the melt of chocolate, the bliss of pure pleasure.

Josh swore under his breath. Her eyes flew open. His expression was hungry. For her.

He reached across the table and slid off her sunglasses. "I want to see your eyes."

And that was all he wanted. He didn't lean across the table to her. Didn't pull her in. A perfect gentleman, as promised.

She was suddenly annoyed at the gentleman act. Even though it was the main reason she felt comfortable being on the date in the first place.

"Go ahead and have some," she said, pushing the cake toward him.

"I'd rather watch you enjoy it." He pushed the plate back toward her.

"No, I'm good."

"You want me to feed it to you?"

"Don't be silly." She refilled her wineglass and took a sip. He did the same and then he dug into the cake. He regularly offered her forkfuls, which she greedily took, closing her eyes in chocolate ecstasy each time.

As they drank, they got chattier, laughing about Mad and her crazy antics as a kid and what Claire knew of her from book club.

She leaned across the table and spoke in a confidential whisper. "She brought this crap tequila with a worm in it and then Hailey tried to make me eat it!" She felt pleasantly buzzed, good wine with good food and excellent company.

He grinned. "Mezcal. It's a novelty and that worm was there solely for Mad's amusement, trust me. She's a bartender, she knows the good stuff."

"Damn, you're right. Sneaky chick." She went to pour more wine and realized it was empty. She held up the bottle. "We finished it."

"There's another bottle," he said, reaching down to the cooler. He stopped. "Maybe we shouldn't have it since we have to drive home after this."

"It's no problem," she said breezily. "I'll call my driver."

"You mean Uber?"

She quickly realized her mistake. "Yes. So handy, that service. Let's drink. You can come back for your car tomorrow. I mean, if you don't mind spending a little more time with me."

"Not at all," he said, his voice gravelly. Sparks of lust shot through her. She hadn't been with a man in a year, by choice, but now…Josh was really doing it for her.

She looked around the empty clearing and had a brilliant idea. "We could have the wine and then camp here to sleep it off." And sleep with each other.

Naked camping. She bit back a giggle.

His eyes widened. "Do they let you do that?"

She lifted her hands to the sky. "Let's find out."

"What about a tent?"

"We'll rough it." She never wanted to go back to civilization. She wanted to stay in this happy bubble until it inevitably popped. She grabbed the blanket from the bench next to her and held it up. "Shelter!"

She went to the grassy clearing and spread the blanket out. It was big enough for two people to sit on, but not big enough for them to sleep on, really. She lay down and her feet hung over the side, the grass tickling her ankles. She propped up on her elbows. "Bring the wine."

He uncorked the wine and joined her, sitting cross-legged next to her. He filled both their glasses. She followed his gaze out to the horizon. The sun was dipping in the sky, streaks of orange and pink against blue. She sipped her wine and found herself studying his profile, the sharp lines of his cheekbones, his angular jaw with the hint of five o'clock shadow. His lips looked extremely kissable.

She set her wineglass in the grass, relaxed and uninhibited enough to make the first move. She stroked his jaw with her fingertips, feeling the rough stubble. "Anyone ever tell you how gorgeous you are?"

He put his hand on top of hers, clasping it warmly, and turned to gaze into her eyes. "Anyone ever tell you how beautiful you are?"

"All the time," she answered honestly. Oops!

"Me too," he said with a laugh. "That never gets

old."

She took his wineglass, set it down next to hers on the ground, and tucked her knees under her, drawing close to him. "I'm thinking about kissing you," she whispered, her fingers sliding into the soft hair at the nape of his neck.

His warm hand cupped her cheek, a ghost of a smile playing over his lips. "I'm thinking that's a good idea."

She closed the distance, her lips brushing against his, bringing a jolt of heat. She pulled back for a moment, a little surprised at the jolt. His deep brown eyes matched her surprise, then morphed into raw desire. She launched herself at him, toppling them both over. The kiss was hot, hungry, out of control as they rolled on the blanket, limbs tangling together. Her hands were all over him, stroking across wide shoulders, down the hard planes of his back, their pelvises pressed together, filling her with an aching desperate need. He wrapped his arms around her, pulling her on top of him, and kissed her some more. Deep, hot, wet kisses that sent her into a frenzy of want. Frustratingly, his hands had yet to roam on her. The gentleman thing suddenly got old.

She tore her mouth away, remembering he wanted clear consent. "Touch me."

He didn't need any more encouragement than

that. He rolled on top of her, holding himself up on his forearms, and then his mouth claimed hers. He slid the strap of her tank to the side and smoothed a caress over her shoulder. She pushed the other strap down and felt her breasts spring free in the warm air. His hand cupped her breast, stroking lightly across the hard tip. She couldn't get enough of him, his mouth, his hard body, his heat. She needed more. A lot more. She'd never ramped up with need like this. She wanted to strip down and have her way with him *right now*.

But before she could do more than grab his ass, he lifted his head and smacked the back of his neck. "As much as I'd love to keep kissing you, I'm getting feasted on by mosquitoes. I don't think this camping idea is going to work."

He got off her, stood, and smacked away mosquitoes in a bunch of places on his neck, arms, and legs. He'd protected her from them, covering her with his body. Whether it was intentional or not, it made her like him even more. Her makeup assistant, Kyra, would have a fit trying to cover a bunch of bug bites before filming. She spent half the movie naked or near-naked.

She slid the tank back in place and adjusted her bra, still turned on and not wanting the date to end. He held a hand out to help her up.

She grabbed his hand and stood. His gaze was hot

and hungry, roaming from her eyes to her lips to her neck and breasts. Then back to her mouth. They slammed together again, his mouth hard and devouring, his hands firm on her hips. Her fingers dug into the soft cotton of the back of his shirt, his heat radiating through her. She wanted more, she wanted raw, she wanted real. Jenny Coleman could have that.

She broke the kiss and met his eyes. "I'm offering my consent." She flushed. She'd never actually said anything like that out loud before. It felt like she was proclaiming her lust for him. But Hailey said that was what he wanted—an affirmation of desire and consent. And her lust was much stronger than any embarrassment over the necessary conversation.

His grip on her hips tightened. "Your consent?"

"You know," she whispered, cheeks flaming. Dammit. Did Hailey just say that as a joke? Augh. The good news was his hand was now on her ass, pressing her firmly against his massive erection. She bit back a moan.

"For what exactly?" he asked.

Her eyes snapped to his. Wow. She didn't think it would be this difficult. She wanted to be Jenny a little longer, and, more importantly, she wanted him. Like an inferno of *gotta have it right now* need. Clearly he wanted her too, but he seemed to really want all the gentleman words before they took this any further. She stifled a sigh. Did she really have to spell it out? She was squirming with embarrassment and lust, being held right up against his hard hot male body. He loosened his hold, his hands moving to her hips and then sliding up, spanning her ribs just shy of her aching, tingling breasts.

She sighed.

He tipped her chin up, his eyes warm and soft. "I don't want any misunderstandings."

Fine. He needed it spelled out in bold letters, then that was what she'd do. "Hailey says you need an affirmation of desire and consent."

He cocked his head like he was listening, but maybe wasn't following. He'd seemed so sharp before, his speech so intelligent and articulate. Did he really not understand?

A tickling of mortification went through her, shoving bold proclamations of lust out the window. Maybe this was—

He grabbed her unexpectedly around the waist, lifting her so they were chest to chest, eye to eye. "What's all this about desire and consent?" he asked in a very serious tone.

"For sex," she whispered.

He grinned. "Can't get more clear than that." He gave her a smacking kiss on the lips. "Magic to my ears."

She beamed. She'd got him. "Music."

His dark brown eyes sparkled with good humor. "That too."

"Can we go to your place? I have a roommate."

"Let's walk to town. There's a few B&Bs there. Then we don't have to worry about driving after all that wine." A bed and breakfast! How quaint!

"Brilliant!" She floated in a haze back through the woods, Josh's fingers entwined with hers. They kept bumping into each other, trying to walk so closely, or maybe that was her because she was a little tipsy. He stopped a bunch of times to kiss her again while she rubbed shamelessly against him.

He stowed the cooler in his car, and a short walk later, they crossed the pedestrian bridge over the river and onto the sidewalks of downtown Greenport. Josh assured her the B&B he had in mind was just a couple of blocks away. She waited outside a drugstore while he thoughtfully bought condoms, not wanting to be seen on any security cameras even in disguise.

He stepped out, bag in hand, gave her a quick kiss, and they continued on their journey to raw primal lust. A horrible thought occurred, one she couldn't let slide. "Are you going to be a gentleman in the bedroom?"

He squeezed her hand gently. "Do you want me to be?"

"No!"

He chuckled. "I love how honest you are. You're the real deal, Jenny."

She swallowed. She wasn't at all. He was the one who was the real deal—honest, down to earth, the kind of guy she would've been with back before she made it big.

But she could still be herself in the bedroom, she reasoned. As long as he didn't know her real name. As long as it was dark. As long as he wasn't a hair grabber. She couldn't worry about that right now. This had to happen. It had been so long since she'd wanted anyone at all. She went up on tiptoe and whispered what she wanted to do to him. He grabbed her hand, practically running down the sidewalk, making her laugh.

He stopped, kissed her breathless, and then pulled her along to an adorable bed and breakfast. She wasn't going to think about tomorrow or the next day. All she wanted was one raw passionate night.

CHAPTER FIVE

Josh was regretting this dinner date as his twin more and more. The restaurant was too posh. He had to wear a damn monkey suit and the portions were tiny. Not only that, Hailey, sitting across from him, looked like a perky princess of sunshine, and he couldn't stop soaking her in. Dammit. The woman was glowing, animated and enthusiastic. She was never like that with him, only for billionaire Jake. With Josh, she was always huffy with her nose in the air.

He might've had a little something to do with that.

She was so easy to rile up, and he couldn't seem to help himself. But tonight, he was being Jake, and she was all smiling enthusiasm to every boring fact he spit out about his fancy lifestyle. He did it just to see how much she was into the money thing and, boy, was she ever. He fought the urge to loosen his tie before he laid it on thick, bragging about his six-thousand-square-foot home with a pool and a view of the bay. How he'd hired the best architect, best interior designer, blah, blah, blah.

"That sounds wonderful," Hailey enthused.

He was both miffed with her rapt attention to all this boring shit and in the throes of unwanted lust. Her white dress was ruffled on top and off-the-shoulder, exposing creamy shoulders that he wanted to sink his teeth into. He hadn't missed the way the dress clung to her perfect body—full breasts, curvy hips and ass, shapely legs. He scowled and pulled out his cell phone. As usual, Hailey had him teetering between two extremes, an uncomfortable feeling for his purposefully laid-back life. "You'll love this," he told her, swiping through the photos until he got to the one of his brother on his huge yacht. He showed it to her.

"Wow! So cool!" she exclaimed. "I've always wanted to try sailing."

Even he knew you didn't sail on a yacht. "It's more like boating. No sail, see?"

She flushed pink all the way to her neck. "Of course. I don't know the first thing about boats. Tell me more about Dat Cloud."

He stifled a groan. More boring shit. *What did you think it would be like impersonating your twin?* Jake had a damn boring job, though the lifestyle wasn't bad. He told her what he could remember about Dat Cloud, including the impressive fact that the top-secret underpinnings of their application still hadn't been replicated successfully anywhere. Though those motherfuckers at competing firms tried. She was all smiles and enthusiasm, so he went on with Dat Cloud's uses both domestically and abroad. He was putting himself to sleep.

Dammit. He'd wanted to teach her a lesson. A big reveal to show her that lowly bartenders were just as good to hang with as gold-plated guys, but she was proving to really like the glitter. That automatically put her out of the running for his brother. Jake had his share of gold diggers. With a perverse sense of justice, he decided not to tell her who he really was at the end of the date. He wasn't a fan of beauty queens looking for the next ladder up to money. Oh, yeah, he'd looked her up. She had multiple tiaras to her name. He hated that whole pageant business. It made women obsessed with their looks. He didn't have to look any further than his own beauty-queen mom bailing on her six kids for greener pastures as a prime example.

She was chattering on now about her dreams of travel. He'd seen more than enough of the world and was happy to plant himself in the sleepy small town of Clover Park.

"Though I confess I haven't made it west of the Mississippi," she said, leaning forward in a conspiratorial whisper. He stared at her soft pink lips. At least they looked soft and probably tasted sweet. He forced his eyes back to hers. "Maybe I could visit you one day in California and see Dat Cloud headquarters." She slapped a hand over her mouth. "That was presumptuous."

"Why the hell not," he said, shoving a microscopic piece of prime rib in his mouth. It came like that, all tiny thin slices in a tiny white ramekin. Most of his plate was white space. "Easy enough with my private jet."

Her light blue eyes widened. "Where do you like to travel?"

"Wherever the wind takes me," he replied dryly.

She tossed her light red hair over one bare smooth shoulder. Raw lust shot through him. He shifted uncomfortably and forced himself to focus on the fact that the dress was probably silk, some expensive designer number. He preferred flannel shirts, worn tees, and ripped jeans. He and Hailey were nothing alike. What was he doing here? Why couldn't he keep away from her?

But his body knew. It was an itch that wouldn't let up, no matter how much he tried to deny it. He couldn't deny her requests to go to weddings, though he made a big deal of it, like it was a hardship on account of the monkey suit and all that lovey-dovey business he had to sit through. The first time she'd asked, three months ago, he'd said she'd have to make it worth his while in an admittedly piss-poor attempt at flirting. She'd countered that she'd only asked him out in a professional capacity and offered cash up front for his time. Feeling like a fool for his uncharacteristic awkwardness with a beautiful woman, he took the cash. And kept taking it for two more weddings and three platonic blind dates whenever she snapped her fingers. He should probably see a shrink or something. Clearly he was insane to want someone that he didn't even like.

She tucked a lock of hair behind her ear in a self-conscious gesture.

Except maybe he kinda did like her.

"That must be nice to have no limits on travel like that," she said, daintily slicing a piece of chicken. Her manners were polished, her movements always graceful and poised. Everything about her said upper-class beauty queen. "Just wherever the wind takes you," she said dreamily. "I'd definitely head to Paris and then Italy, Spain, ooh, maybe Morocco too."

He inclined his head. "Been to all those places." And worse.

"Tell me all about Paris," she said.

"I'd much rather hear where you've traveled." He was sick of hearing himself brag about Jake.

She flushed pink. "It's nothing special."

"Tell me anyway."

She started chattering about Connecticut, a trip to Atlantic City when she turned twenty-one, and a field trip to Washington, DC, with her eighth-grade class, all places within driving distance. Strange. He would've thought with all the pageants and money she'd won, not to mention her fancy designer duds, she would've done a lot of luxury travel. A tickling of unease went through him. Could she afford to pay him for wedding dates and blind dates all in the name of her business? Was that tax deductible? She paid him in cash, and he stuffed it in a shoebox on the top of his closet. To give it back meant admitting he couldn't stop hanging around her, and he'd confess only with a knife to the throat that he took out those other women for a purely platonic blind date just to make her jealous.

He finished his wine in one long swallow as she kept talking. He'd never considered spending her money, even though he was still saving for his dream—a bar with good food, pool tables, and a dance floor with an old-fashioned jukebox. He wouldn't hit up Jake for the funds, and he wouldn't use her money because he needed to know the bar was all his. He consoled himself with the knowledge the money would go back to her one day, he just hadn't worked out how.

He clamped his mouth shut against the questions he had about her and her financial situation, unwilling to learn more about her as Jake. This was fucked up. He'd finish dinner, drop her off, and that would be the end of it.

No more platonic blind dates at her request.

No more weddings either.

He looked away from her bright blue eyes, her pink-tinged cheeks, her rosy mouth, her long neck, her exposed delicate collarbone, and scowled.

He never should've tangled with her in the first place.

~ ~ ~

Hailey could feel her mouth getting away from her, babbling on and on, but Jake was so quiet now, and she'd never been to such a fancy restaurant. There was actually a man just in charge of the wine! She feared the superwealthy patrons would know she was wearing last season's dress. She shopped at the consignment shop in Greenport religiously every Tuesday when they marked stuff down to make room for the next batch of donations. She knew her designers and what would look good on her, even if they were a season or two out of date. She'd grown up poor, the only child of a single mom (a former model turned high-end boutique sales clerk who regularly flaked on work), and had clawed her way up ever since. Beauty pageants had taught her poise and composure, and the winnings had helped pay her way through college.

She was flagging in her enthusiasm. She finished her glass of ridiculously expensive chardonnay that cost more than her entire outfit. For one glass! She scrambled to think of another conversation starter. She'd accepted his invitation for dinner, through a text from Josh, for the rare chance to pick the brain of a really successful businessman. She wanted to know more about his business and how he built it up. She wanted to talk profit and loss, when he'd scaled up with employees, when he'd ramped up investment back in the business, at what point he'd decided to take the company public, but he showed zero interest in the topic. She couldn't believe he ran a global company with so little enthusiasm for the task. If she were to build her wedding planning business as big as she wanted, making it the go-to destination of every bride's dream, why, she'd be gushing!

She hated to admit it, but Jake was kind of…boring. And a little bit braggy about his mansion and his yacht.

She shut up for the first time all night and focused on finishing her dinner of roast chicken, five tiny potatoes, and three baby carrots. The portions were so tiny here. She figured it was to make sure people would have room for dessert. Though she wasn't so sure she wanted to extend dinner. Her mind wandered to the details she had to firm up for the Wilson-Cruz wedding. She stifled a yawn, realized she was being rude, and offered a smile to her boring companion.

He gave her a half-smile, only pulling up one corner of his mouth. He did have nice soulful deep brown eyes. Reminded her of Josh with the depth of intelligence to them, the way he held her gaze as he spoke. He didn't smile as much as Josh did, though. Of course, Josh's smiles were only because he was teasing her, or she was handing him cold hard cash to be her wedding date. Yes, Josh was her paid escort. She needed dependable dates to weddings, and he needed cash. Seriously, she couldn't be a professional matchmaking wedding planner and always show up alone at weddings. She was too busy building a business from the ground up and a secure future for herself to spend any time looking for love. Josh was safe. He understood it was a professional transaction. They'd happened upon the arrangement when she'd desperately needed a date to Julia's wedding, the most important one of her career so far because Julia was a globally bestselling author and movie star Claire would be in attendance. (The guy Hailey was supposed to go with totally flaked.) She'd asked Josh, who'd obviously needed some incentive to attend a wedding—it really was an event more for the bride—so she'd offered cash. He'd said it would come in handy for his own future business. This pleased her. Two businesspeople taking care of business. She was building the foundation of her wedding planning business, and Josh was saving money for the bar he wanted to open one day.

She took a sip of wine. Between the bestselling author and the movie star, Hailey had been sure Clover Park would become *the* wedding destination. Not so much. Business was steady, but hadn't exploded as she'd hoped. In any case, she appreciated Josh's dependability and punctuality. The guys her age, early twenties, were so unreliable. Half the time they didn't show, or they'd show but really late. Josh conveniently lived and worked in town. Also, he was easy on the eyes, though she'd admit it only at gunpoint.

Hanging on the edge of a cliff.

By her fingernails.

Because he was an obnoxious, arrogant cad. Until he got his money, then he was a charming gentleman. See? Cad.

She finished her tiny dinner. Josh was such a charming, gentlemanly paid escort, she'd come up with the idea of loaning him out to singles looking for love, hoping he'd boost their confidence enough to spark a love quest. Not with him, of course, they were both up front with the single ladies that the date would be fun and only one time. It was a mutually beneficial arrangement that she and Josh had.

She finished her wine while Jake dug around for more meat in the tiny ramekin. She felt good about her two-year strong business. Even the bit with Josh. She both hated his teasing at the end of every wedding date and looked forward to it. She'd always been a woman of contradictions. She believed women should be a little mysterious. It was something her mom had taught her at an early age. Though Josh brought out more of her unmysterious practical self. He pushed all her buttons—hot, bothered, and not going there. She was a professional Love Junkie. It said so on her card.

Three months ago, when Josh had been her escort for the first time at Julia and Angelo's wedding, he let slip a little tidbit that he had brothers and that got her pumped because her singles book club desperately needed men! He was suddenly immensely useful to her. Indispensable, really. If she didn't keep up a constant stream of weddings, she'd lose her job. This was her dream gig—planning the happiest day in a couple's life, making sure the event ran smoothly, all while living in her beloved hometown—and she wanted to keep it. Clover Park had the gorgeous mansion and the homegrown businesses to support weddings. The problem was the residents were mostly families. She needed an influx of single men. She already had five eligible single women in book club, some from Clover Park and some from nearby towns, ready and waiting for love. Their happy-ever-afters were in her capable hands.

"Wait!" she'd called after Josh. He was leaving their wedding date because his time was up. "I want to hear about your brothers."

He turned. "Are you extending our date past the originally agreed four hours? That sounds like overtime."

She ignored that obnoxious remark. Like she had to pay him just to talk to her! "Can I meet them?"

"No."

She rushed to his side, eager to know more. "What are their names?"

He ticked them off on his fingers. "No, no, no, and no."

"So there's four of them?"

"Maybe."

"Can't you tell me anything?" she asked in exasperation.

He cocked his head. "What's it worth to ya?"

She checked her purse. Seven dollars left. "Five dollars."

"You insult me."

"Seven."

"Ha!"

She frowned and then immediately corrected to a neutral expression so she wouldn't get frown lines. "That's all I have."

He leaned close. "Well, princess, there are other ways of paying up." The "princess" wasn't a compliment. It was a dig at how perky she was, how goody-goody. She was merely a pleasant person. This obnoxious arrogant cad was making her think of taking up yoga just to keep her cool. *Ohm.* Bastard. As if she had the time.

At the hot look in his eyes, she swallowed hard. She was *not* going to fall into that leading trap of what "other" ways she might pay up. He was just teasing her again, trying to get her worked up, and she refused to take the bait.

He told her anyway. "One kiss for one question answered."

He was a scoundrel. Their arrangement was purely professional. He knew she'd never take him up on that. Right? They'd agreed the wedding date was good for both of their business plans.

She went straight for the questions. Let him think he'd get his devious payment later. "How many brothers? Are they single? And how old?"

He grinned. "That's three questions. That'll cost more, and I want payment up front."

Darn. She'd planned on bailing right after she found out what she needed to know.

He leered at her just to annoy her.

"Fine!" she said, tossing her purse over her shoulder. "Forget it! I'll ask Mad." That was his younger sister, who was in singles book club. They were friends. Sort of.

"Good luck with that," Josh said. "Mad is a vault." His lips played at a smile. "Last chance."

"I'll call you the next time I need your services," she said coolly.

"Bring cash," he said and left.

She blinked, suddenly returning to the present. Jake was standing at her side, waiting for her to get up. She had to stop daydreaming about work. He must've already paid, and she hadn't even noticed.

She stood. "Thank you for dinner."

"You're welcome."

He held her by the elbow with a light and surprisingly warm touch, guiding her out of the restaurant. It was the kind of gentlemanly move Josh always did. She wondered how Josh's date was going tonight with Claire. She kinda wished she were enjoying a quiet little picnic in the woods right about now.

They stepped out onto the sidewalk where the limo they'd arrived in was waiting. Jake must've called the driver while she was daydreaming. The city was busy with people and cars and light, and it made her tired. She just wanted to get home to her cozy basement apartment in Clover Park. It was her woman cave filled with romance novels, romantic movies, scented candles, and stacks of bridal magazines. The furniture was secondhand, the cushions of the floral sofa nice and mushy, and the scarred wood of the coffee table and bookcases felt well loved by the generations. Like she was carrying on history just by having them.

She suddenly realized he was standing very close to her, and he smelled so *good*. Like the warm spice aftershave Josh wore when he bothered to shave. Twins probably favored similar products. She stepped back, a little startled to find she wanted to stay close after that incredibly boring business dinner.

He gazed at her for a long moment, the intense heat in those brown eyes making her breath catch. He'd seemed so standoffish before.

He turned abruptly to open the limo door for her. She got in, careful to keep her dress discreetly tucked around her, and he shut the door behind her.

She powered down the window. "Aren't you coming?"

A muscle ticked in his clenched jaw. Maybe something came up with work while she was in la-la land. "I'll be staying in the city. Goodnight."

"Goodnight," she said. "Thanks again for dinner."

He tapped the roof of the car, and the driver pulled away from the curb. Huh. That was kinda strange. She turned in her seat, watching him, hands in his pockets, walking in the opposite direction.

She faced front. What a night. She watched the bright lights of the city zoom past on the limo ride home and had to admit her paid escort dates with Josh were far superior to having dinner with his twin. One thing she could say about Josh, no matter how much he teased, she was never bored. Not that she thought dinner with Jake was a date. It had been business for her, one entrepreneur to another, talking shop. At least that was what she'd hoped it would be.

She sighed and slid off her heels, flexing her feet. She'd created her dream job herself and here she was two years later, still going strong. And the best was yet to come. Especially once she got Josh to introduce her to all those Campbells! She just hoped they weren't as obnoxious as Josh or as boring as Jake or as hostile as Mad.

Hmm…maybe she needed a new plan.

CHAPTER SIX

Jake forgot about his itchy mosquito bites the moment Jenny boldly stated she wanted to have sex. The consent words had some weird-ass Josh tones to it, and he suspected Josh had been messing with Hailey, who'd innocently passed along the info, but whatever. It worked. He couldn't wait to peel her out of her modest clothes to reveal what he knew would be an amazing body. But first he had to deal with the front desk clerk of the bed and breakfast, an elderly woman who made a big show of lowering her bifocals to observe their only luggage—the nearly transparent plastic bag holding a box of condoms. Jenny wandered to the other end of the hall, admiring a painting of a sailboat. Sure, leave him holding the sex bag in front of the morality police.

He dug out his wallet and snagged a hundred-dollar bill, folding it neatly in half. "Just passing through for the night." He handed the elderly woman the cash in a handshake. "We travel light."

"Of course," she said, tucking the bill in her cleavage. "We'll need payment up front. Breakfast starts at eight a.m."

He paid with his credit card, glad that Jenny was so enthralled with the painting that she wouldn't notice the name on his card.

Finally, he got the key. He crossed back to Jenny. "Let's go."

They hurried upstairs in silence. He opened the door to the room, letting her go first like a gentleman. So far the gentleman thing had worked heavily in his favor, though he knew he couldn't keep it up much longer. Not with the way he wanted her. He stepped into a fussy flowery room—flower wallpaper, flower bedspread, flower throw pillows. So much pink.

"It looks like a flower shop threw up in here," Jenny quipped.

He laughed, headed for the nightstand, and set the condoms there. He crossed back to where she was standing in front of the dresser. She'd removed her cap and was looking in the mirror, smoothing her hair. He wrapped his arms around her from behind, trailing kisses down the side of her neck, breathing her in, vanilla sweetness and sexy woman. She raised her arms, reaching back to hold his shoulders. He gave her a nip on the side of her neck, and she gasped.

"Not too rough," she said in that throaty, husky voice. "Don't leave a mark."

"Why?" He kissed his way back up her neck, gliding his hands up to her breasts, cupping them, full and ripe. He felt himself get harder as her nipples beaded under his hands. He met her green eyes in the mirror, hers were full of desire, her color high, her full lips parted. His control was about to snap. "You got a boyfriend who cares about a bite?"

She turned in his arms and put a hand to his chest, pushing him away. He didn't budge. "No boyfriend," she said. "Here's the deal. No marks and don't touch my hair. If you're good with that, anything goes."

His grip on her loosened in surprise. *Anything?*

She leaned past him to the light switch and turned off the lights. Her arms wrapped around his neck, and she spoke against his lips. "Promise, okay?" Her hands ran down his back and cupped his ass. "No marks, don't touch the hair. Otherwise anything—"

"Deal," he said, lifting her onto the dresser and spreading her legs. He kissed her, suddenly ravenous. She opened for him, and he swept his tongue inside, tasting wine and sweet spicy woman. His pulse pounded in his ears. He couldn't get enough; he wanted to merge with her.

He broke the kiss just long enough to rip off her tank top and undid the bra clasp one-handed. Dim light from the hallway gave him a gorgeous view of full breasts. He slid the bra off her, cupped one breast and took it in his mouth with tight suction. She moaned softly, her hand on his head, keeping him there. He worked the nipple of her other breast, rolling and tugging on it with one hand while he suckled the other. Her head fell back, the open surrender amping him up. He lifted his head, returning to her mouth, their tongues tangling, feverish hot. Sharp need had him scooping her off the dresser. She wrapped her arms and legs tightly around him as he carried her to the bed.

He banged his shin against the wooden frame of the bed. *Ouch!* "I need a little light."

"No! I mean, I'm shy."

She hadn't seemed shy when she had her tongue down his throat, but he didn't have a chance to point that out because she started nipping and licking his neck aggressively, and he knew this first time was going to be fast and furious. He set her on the bed, stripped out of his clothes, and then slid her shorts and panties off. He wished he could see her. The light from the hallway didn't reach the bed.

He joined her and the rest was a hot blur, her hands were all over him, and then she was tugging at his shoulders, pulling him on top of her. He slid a hand between her legs to find her bare, hot, and soaked with desire. Fuck. He was painfully hard, blue steeler here, but he wanted to bring her pleasure first. He stroked her some more, loving her throaty moans even as his blood surged through his veins, urging him to take. But then she wrapped her hand around his throbbing cock, and he couldn't wait. Neither could she.

"Fuck me, Josh," she said in a throaty voice that both wound him tight and alarmed him. He should tell her he was Jake.

She kissed him roughly, biting down on his lower lip. Later. He'd tell her later. He thrust his fingers inside her, and she gasped into his mouth. Tight, so tight. He thrust some more with his fingers, trying to ready her, swallowing her moans. He shifted his hand, cupping her more firmly on the inside, letting the heel of his hand rub against her. She went off, her hips jerking straight off the mattress, a cry wrenched from her throat. He slid his hand from her, and she sank down, her legs open and relaxed.

He snagged the box on the nightstand, tore it open, and got a condom on in record time. He returned to her, settled between her legs, and drove home in one swift thrust. She cried out. Fuck. She clasped tightly around him. He'd never been so turned on. He pulled nearly all the way out and slid in slowly, drawing a moan from her. She lifted her hips, and he went deep.

"Yes," she hissed, wrapping her legs around his waist, and something in him snapped.

He thrust hard, over and over, pumping with a ferocity he'd never felt in his life. Possession. White-hot need. Pure animal fucking. She met him thrust for thrust, angling up for him, taking him deep. He couldn't have slowed down if he wanted to; she was tight, hot, grabbing his ass, urging him on. She stiffened and then cried out, shuddering around him. He pumped once more before he came so hard, his vision dimmed and his ears rang. Whoa.

He dropped his head and pressed his lips to the side of her neck.

"Fuck me, Josh, you're awesome," she said cheerfully, slapping him on the shoulder.

He groaned and rolled onto his back. He wished she'd stop calling him that. The Josh thing was dimming the awesome. "You too," he said hoarsely.

She rolled to her side and rubbed his chest. "How long until you can do it again?"

He smiled sleepily in the dark. "Wake me in an hour." Then he conked out.

She woke him as promised. Twice more that night, both times sliding a condom onto him, climbing on board, and riding him hard. He fucking loved it. She was wild and free and just as into it as he was. Just as the sun was coming up, he zonked out in the sleep of the dead.

When he woke hours later, she was gone.

He sat up, an inkling of dread coursing through him. She wouldn't really leave without saying goodbye, would she? Not after that amazing night.

"Jenny?" he called. He got out of bed and checked the bathroom. Nothing. Did a quick check of the room for any sign of her. She really had left without saying goodbye. He didn't have her number. That couldn't be the end. That night meant something. So raw and real and passionate.

He snagged his cell and Googled her. There was no Jenny Coleman in Connecticut. He tried New York. He found a masseuse that didn't look anything like Jenny. He clicked through several more searches and found nothing close to her looks or location. He didn't know the name of her business. He didn't know anything about her except that she was in the book club. He'd text Josh for the info. Should've thought of that first.

He started to type and stopped himself. Maybe Jenny really only wanted one night. She had reminded him of that during their hike. She had a life here. His life was in California.

He put his cell away and told himself to put Jenny out of his mind. It was fun. End of story.

He snagged his clothes from the floor and sank heavily onto the bed. It smelled like sex. It smelled like Jenny. The feel of her satiny smooth skin, the sound of her moans, her taste, her tight, welcoming body. How was he supposed to forget that?

He dressed and then he just sat there, elbows on his knees, debating texting Josh for her number. He wanted to see her again. It wasn't often he connected with a woman like that—the passion between them, the easy conversation on their hike. Her open down-to-earth way of talking. Her throaty sexy voice. Her curvy sweet-smelling body.

He quickly texted Josh. His brother didn't know her number, but said he'd find out. Hours later, Josh had nothing. No phone number, no work info, no link to her at all.

She couldn't have vanished, could she?

CHAPTER SEVEN

Claire had regrets. Her regrets had regrets. A never-ending chain of *why did I ever agree to meet Josh* regrets because now she couldn't get the man out of her head.

She returned to work, quickly inundated with demands for her attention, yet Josh kept coming back to her in flashes of memory. His smile that crinkled his warm brown eyes. His gentlemanly manners that, thankfully, went out the window once they got to the bedroom. His kisses that made her dizzy with lust. She worked long hours with no downtime in a futile effort to stop thinking about Josh. Finally on Friday, she got a welcome distraction, a text from Hailey inviting her to a book club meeting that night. Yes. This was what she needed. More time with her new friends. But then another text came through, making her grip the cell phone tighter.

Josh wants to see Jenny again.

She knew she should say no. It wouldn't be fair to

Josh to continue the lie. And, if she told him the truth, he'd be angry that she'd pretended. An angry scorned lover was not what the Claire Jordan image needed. He could do serious damage in the press. She wished there were some way she could see him again. Dammit. She texted Hailey back.

No time for Jenny date. Very busy. I can only manage book club.

Same place, same time?

That works for me.

Ciao!

Claire smiled. *Ciao.*

Work dragged the rest of the afternoon probably because she couldn't wait to meet up with everyone back in the hotel lounge. It seemed like everything and everyone was against her getting there. Blake was throwing a hissy fit about his hairdresser being out sick. The new girl, who Claire thought did just as good a job, was nervous, which made her take longer, which pissed Blake off, making the poor girl more nervous. And even though Claire switched him to her guy, Blake's irritation lingered, bleeding into his performance, making what should have been a tender scene between him and Mia into something with an edge that would only confuse the audience. On top of that, the circuit in the kitchen blew out when one of their camera operators plugged in a coffeemaker. At least that was just a matter of resetting the circuit breaker in the basement and figuring out, by trial and error, which outlets could hold the load of cameras, lights, monitors, and laptops.

Finally she made her escape only to hit heavy traffic on the expressway. She wanted to scream. After a week of frenzied working hours, trying to forget Josh, she needed to relax with her friends.

By the time Frank escorted her through the back entrance of the hotel and up the private elevator to the private lounge, everyone was already there. The women were chatting and sipping wine that they must've brought themselves because Claire had been too busy to arrange anything. Bags of potato chips and tortilla chips were being passed around the circle of women. The normalcy of it all made her tear up. "Hi, sorry I'm late."

"She's here!" Hailey exclaimed. "You must be exhausted after working all day. Have a seat."

Claire dropped into the chair Hailey indicated in the circle of plush chairs and sofa. Charlotte, next to her, handed her the bag of potato chips.

She grabbed a handful of chips and passed it over to Mad on her other side. "Thanks," she said around a chip. "I'm starving."

A moment later, Hailey appeared at Claire's side and gave her a plastic tumbler full of white wine.

"Thanks," Claire said. "It's so good to see you guys."

"You too," Hailey said, taking a seat across the circle from Claire on the sofa, where three women—Lauren, Ally, and Carrie—were already squished. Lauren, a sweet teacher with long light brown hair, got up and took the floor.

"Oh, no, you don't," Claire said. "Here, Laur, take my chair." The woman was too damn accommodating.

"It's okay," Lauren said. Claire was about to insist, but then Mad got up, stomped over to the plastic chairs on the other side of the room, and carried one over next to the sofa.

"Sit," Mad ordered.

Lauren sat.

Mad returned to her seat and peered over at Claire. "I heard you and Josh hit it off. He's asking about you."

"He's great," Claire said, in what she hoped was a calm voice considering how painful it was to know she'd never see him again. "But I won't be seeing him anymore. I don't want to keep pretending."

Mad nodded her approval. "Good."

Claire took a long drink of wine. The room fell silent, everyone staring at her like she was supposed to say something more about her Josh date. For some reason, she wanted to keep the details to herself. It was a special memory she'd always cherish. "Are we talking about the next book? Anyone read *Gone with the Wind*?"

Hailey smiled indulgently at Claire. "First order of business is how was your date with Josh? We want details!"

Mad fidgeted in her seat. "Please, no gory details, he is my brother."

Claire pasted on a polite smile. "I was just telling Mad we had a nice time, and I very much enjoyed the gentleman treatment." And the nongentleman treatment too. She flushed hot, remembering.

"So-o-o…" Hailey said, "do you want to see him again?"

Claire shook her head. "I don't want to pretend anymore. I'll end up hurting him."

"But you liked him?" Hailey asked.

"Did you kiss him?" Carrie, a sweet innocent young nurse with glasses, asked.

Kiss, grope, fuck. Mmm-hmm.

"Was there a spark?" Lauren asked hopefully.

"Sparks are so important," Ally, a bubbly young blonde woman, said with a dreamy sigh. The women all agreed.

Claire's mind flashed back to his glorious mouth and hands and body. And before that, on their date, the warmth in his eyes and words and touch. She stifled her own sigh of longing. "More than a spark," she admitted. "More like an entire Fourth of July fireworks display."

"Damn," Charlotte muttered. "I never got that feeling from Josh, and I've flirted with him a bunch of times at Garner's."

The other women agreed that Josh always flirted and fireworks had never erupted for any of them. Except Hailey, who was quiet. And Mad, who rolled her eyes.

"So you had fireworks, had a great date, and that's it?" Ally asked. "Goodbye forever?"

"That's so sad," Lauren said. Her sympathetic eyes depressed the hell out of Claire. She hated wanting what she couldn't have.

"It is sad," Claire admitted. "But I'm moving on and—"

"Lame-o," Ally sang.

Claire bristled. "I'm trying to do the right thing. There's no sense in continuing a lie."

The women argued whether it was better to see where things went and then admit the truth or just shut the whole thing down. Claire bit into a potato chip. It didn't matter what they said, she was done. She had to be.

"Moving on," Claire said after she finished her handful of chips and the conversation had circled back around to the importance of honesty. "Does everyone have a cocktail dress they can wear for the corporate party scene next Wednesday? You all did get the email from my assistant, right?" She'd invited the book club to play extras in the movie. She knew they were big fans of the Fierce trilogy.

Hailey spoke up. "Claire, this is the first time Josh has ever asked for a second date. He must really like you. At least talk to him. Let him down easy if you're not going to see him again."

Claire ground her teeth and then quickly loosened her jaw, mindful of not destroying thousands of dollars' worth of dental work required for the perfect Hollywood smile. "I'm not Jenny. There's no future. I probably shouldn't have gone out like that in the first place."

Hailey leaned forward, her pale blue eyes locked on Claire's. "When was the last time you had a lot of fun with fireworks-level sparks on a first date? That doesn't happen often."

"Or at all," Charlotte chimed in.

The women had to agree.

It *was* rare. Josh had been wonderful. But what was she supposed to do? She couldn't keep pretending to be someone she wasn't. And she couldn't be herself and risk his anger and the inevitable fallout in the press at this critical time for the Fierce trilogy movies. She'd sunk every last dime into the movies. If the first movie flopped, her production company was done. She knew damn well that beauty faded and good roles for women over thirty (she was twenty-nine) were hard to come by. It was why she'd started her own production company in the first place, to keep her profile high. Even with that kind of creative control, she knew as she aged, she would be less marketable. American audiences worshipped youth and beauty in their actresses. The time for her career was now.

She took a deep breath, trying to ease the ache of longing in her chest. What she really needed was not some romantic happy ending, but friendship. *Look around, you have that. Don't ask for more.*

She surprised even herself when she admitted, "I've been thinking about him a lot." She looked around at her friends gathered close with varying levels of concern and a few smiles. "I didn't expect that."

"I think it's wonderfully romantic," Ally said, her blond bangs bobbing along in time with her head.

Mad frowned. "Don't string him along. Cut ties so he can move on."

"In person or by phone," Hailey said. "Up to you. But Mad's right, if he really cares about you, he deserves closure."

Claire blew out a breath, knowing Hailey was right. He did deserve closure, but she didn't think a text or phone call would be enough after the night they'd had together. Her friends didn't know how far things went, and she didn't want to share. She had to be Jenny again so she could explain to Josh that she couldn't do a relationship. She'd have to come up with some excuse.

"I'll pretend to be Jenny one last time," Claire said.

Hailey clapped.

Mad spoke up. "Just don't lead him on. Be fair."

Hailey spoke in a reassuring tone. "You're doing the right thing. Let him down with a nice it's not you, it's me. Because it is, right? I mean, it's because you're Claire Jordan not because of Josh. I mean, he is pretty easy to spend time with." She pasted a smile on. "And you said yourself there was a spark."

"Moving on," Mad said. "Tell us the latest with *Fierce Longing*."

Claire gave them an update on the scene they'd just finished and the unfortunate injury the stunt double had on his motorcycle. They were still scrambling to find someone else for Monday's shoot, only three days away.

Mad piped up. "My brother Ty does stunts."

Claire turned to her. "Motorcycle stunts?"

"Ty's your guy," Mad said. "He just wrapped a movie in the city."

"Union?"

"Yup."

"Give me his info and have him contact my assistant. If he can be at the estate by eight a.m. call, he's hired. Wait." Claire sighed. "You have a picture, height, and weight? We need someone close to Blake's body type."

Mad pulled her cell phone from the large pocket in her cargo shorts. She tapped the screen and swiped a few times before holding it up. "That's him."

"That works," Claire said. "My assistant will set it up."

Hailey peeked over. "Dang."

"Lemme see," Charlotte said.

Mad handed the phone over to Charlotte. "Dang is right," Charlotte said. "I'd do him."

Julia wiggled her fingers for the phone, and the women passed it around, murmuring in agreement over Charlotte's assessment.

Hailey perked up. "You want a date, Charlotte? A personal trainer and a stunt double. Two very physical people. Could be a match!"

Charlotte shook her head. "Girl, you need to stop. I know you're seeing wedding bells everywhere, but real life doesn't work that way."

"Chicken," Hailey returned.

After that, Claire called for some takeout for everyone and shifted the conversation to what was going on in their lives. But some part of her was already imagining seeing Josh again. What she'd say as Jenny. She couldn't help but wonder if he would make it difficult. If he would press for another passionate night.

She wasn't sure she could resist him. She'd have to keep her distance, have a civil conversation, and say goodbye.

It was her own damn fault for playing at normal. Now she had to make things right, no matter how painful it was.

~ ~ ~

Jake tried not to think too hard about the fact that he was bailing on a party with multiple potential business contacts and scads of beautiful women just to jet back home in the hopes of finding Jenny. But he'd let himself into Josh's apartment late Friday night, and now here he was on Saturday with Josh driving them in his convertible to the park in Eastman for the usual basketball game with the guys.

He hoped the game would get his pent-up frustration out. Josh had no more info on Jenny. He suspected Josh was dicking around, halfheartedly asking Hailey about Jenny while he teased her, getting her worked up for his own perverse pleasure.

Josh made the turn onto the road leading into the

park. "Would you lighten up already? You're like a black cloud in the car."

Jake scrubbed a hand over his face. He couldn't lighten up because he couldn't stop thinking about *her*. "How can she have no digital footprint? I can't find her online and you know I can find anybody."

"I can't believe you flew back home for a second date."

"Which I don't have."

Josh jabbed a finger at him. "You're like obsessed or something."

"Sorry I can't be like you and pretend I don't care."

Josh made the turn into the parking lot. "You fucked her, didn't you?"

He clenched his jaw. "It wasn't like that."

Josh parked and gave him a skeptical look. "I told Hailey you wanted to see Jenny again, and that was a no-go."

Jake's mouth set in a grim line. "I need to see her face-to-face, none of this going through other people. I think if we saw each other again, talked, she'd remember how great it was."

"Where exactly do you see this going? You can't pretend to be me forever. Eventually you have to run your empire."

"I don't know. I just know I'm not done. We're

not done."

Josh shook his head, snagged his water bottle, and got out of the car.

Jake grabbed his water and followed. "Where does the book club meet?"

Josh let out a loud breath of *shut the fuck up*.

The park was just like he remembered. A baseball field in the distance with bleachers, open grassy area, and the blacktopped area with painted lines for two basketball courts. It was a warm day, the first weekend of October, the trees still green with bits of yellow and red popping here and there. They approached the court where a bunch of the guys were doing layups, and a woman with light red hair in a high ponytail all in pink—pink headband, pink tank top, pink shorts, and pink high-tops—dribbled a ball in really high bounces.

"Who's the girl?" Jake asked under his breath.

Josh went stock-still. "What is *she* doing here?"

They got to the edge of the blacktop, where Mad met up with them. "Hey, Jake! I didn't know you came home again." She socked him on the shoulder. He pulled her in for a one-armed hug and ruffled her hair.

"Hi, Josh! Hi, Jake!" the pink woman called, waving and heading straight for them. Hailey. The woman Jake supposedly took out to a top restaurant in the city. Josh had been tight-lipped about the whole thing, saying only they went their separate ways after dinner.

"Did you tell her?" Jake asked Josh under his breath.

"Tell her what?" Mad asked.

"No," Josh said, shifting uneasily from foot to foot like he might make a break for it.

Mad leaned in and lowered her voice. "She wanted to play. She sucks, so go easy on her, okay?"

"She's on your team," Josh said.

Mad swore. "I *knew* you'd say that."

Hailey bounded to their side. She turned to Jake and smiled politely. "Nice to see you again, Jake."

He was surprised Hailey knew which twin he was right away. Jake had on a T-shirt and basketball shorts same as Josh. Of course, there were some differences. Jake's shirt was designer and new; Josh's was worn and faded. Jake only had light stubble, and his twin had a couple days' growth.

Jake smiled, about to have some fun at his twin's expense. "You too. Dinner was great." At Josh's dark look, he added, "*Really* great. We should go out—*oof.*" Josh elbowed him hard. Worth it.

"You went out with Jake?" Mad barked.

Hailey smiled politely at Jake and then turned to Mad. "Yes, it was a business dinner. We talked about

Dat Cloud."

Mad socked her on the shoulder.

"Ow!" Hailey exclaimed and socked her back. "Stop treating me like one of your guy friends! Women don't punch each other."

Mad grinned. "When did this happen?"

"We'll talk later," Hailey said, giving him and Josh a sunny smile. "Ready to get your butts kicked? Mad's been teaching me *mad* skills." She grinned at her own joke.

Mad rolled her eyes.

"Why are you here?" Josh asked Hailey point blank. "Planning some future weddings?"

She threw an arm around Mad's shoulders. "Mad and I are friends. I want to experience her favorite thing. Sports."

Mad blushed and then snarled at Josh, "Don't be a dick."

Josh headed toward the court. Jake followed behind with Hailey and Mad, wanting to ask Hailey about Jenny.

Hailey turned to Mad. "So Campbell order by age is Jake, Josh, Ty, Alex, Logan, and then you."

"Yup," Mad said.

"And now all the Campbells are here," Hailey said. "Who are we missing from the brothers from another mother?"

Jake chuckled. She sounded so formal about their blood brothers.

Mad sighed. "I told you already. Would you like us all to wear name tags?"

"No, no. I'm very good with names." Hailey pointed at the guys still doing layups, ticking their names off as she pointed to each one. "Ethan, Ben, Marcus. Zach's missing. Did I get it right?"

"You get a gold star," Mad said dryly. She took off and stole the ball from Marcus, who was tall and wide, coming in under his arm and catching him by surprise. She shot from center court and the ball went in with a swish. A brief smile flashed on her face before she retrieved the ball and started dribbling with some fancy footwork, showing off.

Hailey tapped her pink fingernail against her pink lips. "Wait, I think we're missing another one. That only makes four non-Campbell men." She turned to him. "Right?"

"Parker," Jake said. "He's overseas with the air force. She doesn't like to talk about him because, you know, she worries."

"They're close?" Hailey asked.

"Course. We grew up together."

"No, I mean romantically."

He felt queasy just thinking that. None of their friends ever crossed that line. That was the rule. Ty, in particular, had made sure Park knew Mad was off-limits because Park had always gone out of his way to include her in their games when the rest of them thought she was nothing but a shrimp who made them lose. Damn, they were jerks back then. It couldn't have been easy being the youngest and the only girl. He watched Mad shoot another swishing basket and then trash-talk Marcus. Hell, it couldn't have been all bad because look at her now. She was a great athlete, strong and confident.

"Hey, Wonder Twin," Ty, his younger brother by two years, said as he jogged over to him. He was a bulkier version of Jake with a buzz cut, dark tan, and a white T-shirt with the sleeves cut off to show off his bulging muscles and tribal tattoos. Ty grabbed him in a hug that involved a lot of pounding on the back. That was Ty. Very physical. It was why he was drawn to stunt work. "Two weekends in a row, Jake? Sounds like a woman."

Hailey let out a weird squeak, flushed bright pink, and ran over to Mad.

"What's the deal with her?" Ty asked, his gaze following Hailey's ass. He turned back to Jake. "Who's she with?"

"Mad."

"I know Mad said that, but…"

"You don't think Mad could have a friend like

her?"

Ty turned to watch Mad trying to teach Hailey how to dribble with her fingertips while Hailey kept complaining about it messing up her nail polish. He turned back. "No."

"Stranger things have happened," Jake said. Like Mad being in a romance book club. He kept that little jewel to himself for revenge against Mad's next prank or leverage, whichever came up first.

Ty rubbed his scruffy jaw. "You here for Hailey?"

"No."

"Cool. As long as she's not on my team. She doesn't even know it's called a point. She keeps saying she's going to score a goal."

They chuckled quietly.

"Come on," Ty said, pulling his shirt over his head. "We're skins. Five on six. The girls are shirts, six on their team to make up for Miss Pink. You call the other three since you're the visitor."

Jake pulled his shirt off, tossing it on the grass. "Josh—"

"Twin freak," Ty said.

They always picked each other because they worked flawlessly together without needing to say a word. The guys broke them up most of the time because the teams were better balanced that way. Jake lowered his voice. "He doesn't want to be on her team."

They both knew what "her" they were referring to. Mad was really good at basketball, despite being the shortest at five foot four. She had speed on her side and great shooting skills. Probably all those hours she put in shooting hoops by the garage when they were kids.

"Fine," Ty muttered. "You, me, Josh, who else?"

He eyed the prospects. He knew all their flaws, all their plays. He picked two of their friends. "Ethan and Marcus." Ethan was a cop, in tip-top shape. Marcus was former varsity basketball in high school.

"Yes!" Ty barked and jogged over to the guys, telling them how it was going to be.

"Why's he get to pick?" Mad asked. "Jake's home the least. I should get to pick since I brought someone new."

"Yeah," Hailey said, chin in the air.

Josh groaned.

Ethan and Marcus took their shirts off and Hailey stared, seeming to be in awe of their pecs and washboard abs. Man, Ethan had a twelve-pack going on or something. Get a life. Josh made a big show of taking off his shirt, but Hailey didn't give him a second look. It was hysterical.

Josh and Alex faced off at center, brothers about the same height, same laid-back attitude. Except Josh was unusually aggressive today, smacking the ball away and over to Marcus. Awesome. The more aggressive one of them got, the rest got into it too. Testosterone rush.

He dove into the fray. Running and body checking and sweating his balls off, careful to avoid the delicate-looking Hailey. Though she didn't shy away from the intense game, frequently jumping in and trying to get the ball. Josh let her once—so fucking obvious they all groaned—but then Ty immediately stole it. Mad passed her the ball a couple of times. Once Hailey threw at the wrong net and they all cheered her on. Mad cursed them out. The other time Hailey tossed it right back to Mad, who scored.

Final score: Skins 90, Shirts 40.

They headed for the metal bleachers nearby to sit for a few minutes and hydrate. Hailey produced a cooler, wheeling it over to them. "I brought Gatorade and orange slices. Help yourself."

She opened it, and they all went for it, thanking her profusely. That was a real nice gesture. They all settled back on the bleachers with their refreshing loot.

Jake took a seat next to Hailey and Mad.

"Thanks for including me today, even though I stink," Hailey said.

"You weren't that bad," Mad said generously.

"You did all right," Jake said.

"Thank you," Hailey said, taking a sip of Gatorade. She didn't really need to hydrate. She didn't even look like she'd broken a sweat. "Where's Josh?"

Mad jerked her thumb behind her where Josh was sitting on the top row of the bleachers. Hailey gestured for him to come down and sit with them.

Josh pulled his shirt on and took a drink of Gatorade.

She gestured again.

He gestured for her to come up to him.

She gestured frantically and all the guys turned to grin at Josh.

"You've been summoned!" Ty called.

They all laughed.

"Shut up," Josh said, stepping his way down to them. He stood a row behind them, towering over Hailey. "What?"

Jake scooted down to make room for Josh next to Hailey. Josh didn't move, and Ty gave him a shove. Josh shoved Ty back and sat next to Hailey.

"Jenny would like to meet with you if you're free tomorrow," Hailey said. "At Baldwin Park."

Jake's ears perked up.

"Yeah, I could do that," Josh said. "How's morning?"

"Afternoon," Jake said. "We've got that thing in the morning." He needed time to make plans.

Josh turned to him. Jake mouthed one. Josh turned back to Hailey. "How's one?"

"Good," Hailey said briskly. "I'll pass along the message. She was busy today."

"Great," Josh said. "Can't wait to see her again."

Mad stomped down the bleachers and tossed her orange peels in the garbage.

Hailey let out a little sigh. "You really like her, huh?"

"Yeah," Josh said, not all that convincingly.

"That's nice," Hailey said, nodding at the same time like she was trying to convince herself how nice it was.

Josh raised a brow, and Jake elbowed him. "Yeah," Josh said.

Mad returned and flopped down next to Hailey.

Josh's eyes went to half-mast, his poker face. "How'd your date go with Jake?"

Mad leaned forward. "Yeah. I want to hear this too."

Hailey flushed pink. "It wasn't a date. We talked business."

"I guess Jake thought it was a date," Josh said.

Jake glared at him.

Mad laughed. "Friend zoned, Jake!"

Hailey shot Jake an apologetic look. "I'm sorry. I didn't mean to give the wrong impression."

Jake held a hand up. "No problem. I get it."

"You weren't attracted to him at all?" Josh asked with an edge to his voice.

Hailey stared straight ahead. "That's very rude of you to ask, especially in front of him."

"Yeah, Josh," Mad said. "What's your deal? Come on, Hailey." Mad climbed down the bleachers and Hailey followed.

Jake shot Josh an amused look, but his brother didn't notice. He was watching Hailey.

She grabbed the handle of the wheeled cooler and addressed the group. "It was nice meeting you all. Thanks again for letting me play."

"Keep practicing," Ty called. "You'll get there."

"Come back anytime," Ethan said with a leer.

Hailey beamed. "Bye!"

"Bye, guys," Mad said. They hollered bye to the women.

Jake turned to Josh as soon as Hailey was out of earshot. "I can't believe you didn't tell her."

"It didn't come up."

"You mean she didn't want you, so you let her think it wasn't you."

"No," Josh snapped. "I just…she was too into the money thing."

Jake shook his head. "She was talking business. You said she had a business plan, that she's ambitious—"

"Just shut up. You got your date. Now you can stop nagging me."

Jake grinned. "See? It paid off to jet home for a second date. Score."

A weight lifted off him. Things were heading in the right direction.

CHAPTER EIGHT

Claire showed up as Jenny, cap pulled low over her shaded eyes, at the appointed meeting place, a quiet park in Clover Park. Hailey had arranged everything for Sunday when Claire had the day off. From the park, it was a quick trip to Hailey's apartment for a debriefing (most likely Claire sharing and Hailey caring) and then back to the city. Aside from a few preschoolers playing on the nearby playground, no one seemed to notice Claire sitting on a bench under an oak tree. She remembered a time in her life when she would've given anything for someone to notice her, to make her feel like somebody, and when she finally achieved that, how gratifying it was, how exhilarating. Now here she was right back to square one *by choice*. Funny how priorities changed.

She saw Josh approaching in a T-shirt, jeans, and sneakers, looking down to earth and real. She'd almost started to think she'd dreamed him up. Nothing glossy about him, but that was part of his appeal. He carried a bouquet of bright yellow flowers. She stood, her heart racing. She hadn't realized how much she'd missed seeing him. A week of replaying their day and night together had brought her to this moment, nearly trembling with excitement.

He stopped in front of her and grinned. "These are for you."

She took the flowers—daisies, tulips, and carnations—and breathed them in. "Thank you." Then she remembered the purpose of this meeting. "You want to have a seat?" She gestured to the bench.

He gazed at her warmly, dipping his head to look under her cap. "It's so good to see you again."

"You too," she breathed.

He smiled and crinkles formed in the corners of his eyes. "I have something planned. Somewhere I want to take you."

"Oh. But I—"

"My lady," he said, crooking his arm for her to take. She stared at his arm, tan and solid. The gentleman manners again. She never got that from anyone.

She took his arm, the rightness of the gesture surprising her. "Where are we going?"

He headed back toward the parking lot. "A tour on the Hudson river. I borrowed a boat from a friend.

We can see the city, go around the Statue of Liberty too."

That sounded amazing. But—

"Josh, I really need to tell you something."

"We'll talk after the boat ride. I just want to show you a good time. Have you ever seen the city from the water?"

She hadn't. By car, helicopter, and plane, but not by boat. She shook her head.

"It's a blast," he said. "You'll love it."

She dropped her hold on his arm. "We should talk—"

"Later. Okay?" He stopped and gave her a quick kiss on the cheek. "I do want to talk, but first I want to have fun."

She met his warm brown eyes, already melting, but she still needed to do the right thing. "I'm just not sure if we should go on another date. I'm not ready for a relationship."

"Just give me a chance. One boat ride. You can do that, can't you?" He leaned down and peered at her under her cap. "Do you have somewhere you need to jet off to?"

She laughed. "No." Jenny probably didn't jet off anywhere.

"Then it's settled."

She caved. Mostly because she longed to be Jenny

with Josh one last time. And he was so set on taking her on a boat trip. Besides, he'd already borrowed the boat. It wasn't like they'd be hooking up.

He took her hand and gave it a gentle squeeze. "Lucky for you, I'm an expert boat guy. Captain, I mean. You can call me Captain."

She laughed. "I remember how modest you are. You're also an amazing big brother—"

"The best. And expert paddleboarder." He grinned unrepentantly.

"Okay, but if I get wet, you're going to be called something much worse than foxy."

"Don't you dare call me cute." He raised his lip in a snarl. "Kiss of death."

"I just might." She pulled out her cell, smiling. "Hold on." She quickly texted Hailey where she'd be and then she fell into the joy of being Jenny.

The boat ride was amazing or maybe that was the company. The boat was a light speedy craft made for six people at most. But it was just them. Josh was at the wheel and she stood next to him, enjoying the view, the sunshine, and fresh air. He had sunscreen, snacks, and drinks on the boat. She was glad she'd worn a cap to keep her wig in place and the sun off her face. They waved to the Statue of Liberty and to a few other passing boats. They ate trail mix and drank lemonade. She felt drunk with happiness. The exhilarating freedom out on the water, finally being with Josh again. He didn't kiss her or touch her more than a hand squeeze. It was just pure fun with no heavy expectations.

Of course, eventually they had to go back to shore and face reality. But for the next three hours, she was Jenny and it was glorious. Finally Josh pulled back to the dock and tied up the boat.

He helped her off like the gentleman he was. "I was starting to think I was never going to see you again. I'm glad you came today."

"Me too."

"You hungry? There's this great Irish pub. We could grab a drink and some dinner and talk."

"Perfect."

The pub was near the waterfront and crowded. Josh got a big welcome from the bartender, who came out from behind the bar to give Josh one of those guy handshake hugs. She gave the man a shy Jenny hello, careful to keep her head down, tilted away from the crowd. They were shown to a back booth away from the noisy bar. The lighting was dim and made it feel cozy. Within a few minutes they had two beers and a basket of chips.

They talked easily, picking up right where they'd left off. Josh was warm and funny, giving her the whole hilarious story of Hailey playing basketball. By the time they finished their meal, she was dreading goodbye. She didn't want the day to end. And she still needed to explain that they couldn't see each other again.

As if he sensed her darkening thoughts, he reached across the table and took her hand. "I want your number." He squeezed her hand gently. "I want to see you again."

She never gave out her number. Only a select few had it—her family, a few work people, Hailey, and Julia. She took a deep breath, knowing she finally had to end things.

"Josh, I had a really fun time today. And I just want to be clear…" She swallowed over the lump in her throat. She really hated hurting him. "Hailey told me you don't usually have a second date. And I really enjoyed it, but—"

"I really like you." He searched her eyes. "I know it's not one-sided. I can see it in your eyes, hear it in your voice, feel it—"

"No. I'm sorry." Her eyes stung with unshed tears. He was just so damn wonderful, but the person he wanted didn't exist. He wanted a sweet small-town girl. She wasn't sweet and hadn't been small town in a very long time.

She gently extricated her hand from his grasp. "I just don't feel the same way. It's not you. You're wonderful. I really mean that."

"Bull."

She sputtered at the harshness in his tone. "I'm sorry?"

His eyes were hard and direct. "Don't feed me a line. Tell me the truth. Why do you want to ignore what we have between us? Two kick-ass dates, one crazy-good night, and then goodbye? If I have to say goodbye, I want the truth."

She licked her lips nervously. It was hard to fake this when every part of her wanted to reach out, grab hold of him, and never let go. She took a deep breath. "I'm just not ready for a relationship."

"Bull."

"What do you want me to say?" she cried, struggling to keep it together. "I'm trying to be nice."

"Fuck nice."

She blinked back tears. Josh was reacting just as she'd feared. A spurned and angry ex could damage the Claire Jordan image in devastating ways. She didn't want to lie anymore, pretending to be someone she wasn't, but it was clear she couldn't risk telling him the truth.

She closed her eyes, pulling herself back into character. She met his hard stare and said in an even tone, "I'm sorry. We can't see each other anymore."

He clenched his jaw, looking extremely pissed off,

but said nothing.

She stood, took one step toward the door, and stopped next to him. "Goodbye," she said softly.

He didn't respond.

She bit her quivering lower lip, told herself to move, but she only managed one step when his hand shot out, wrapping around her wrist, holding her there. His hold was warm and firm, sending her pulse thrumming through her, all of her senses heightened, alert and aware, suddenly craving more of his heat, his touch, his—dammit. She couldn't believe she could get turned on by a wrist hold from the man she was trying to say goodbye to.

She risked a look at him. His expression was unreadable, hard and devoid of emotion.

"Please let go," she said softly, though some part of her wished he'd never let her go.

"Goodbye, whoever you are," he said and let her go.

She bolted, her heart racing. He knew she was faking. She burst through the door and walked briskly uptown toward her hotel. After a block, she glanced back. He wasn't following her. She was both relieved and disappointed. He didn't know who she was, she was pretty sure, but he suspected something was off. He should suspect. Obviously she couldn't pretend anymore. She was screwing it up, her performance permanently flawed by her longing for him.

She pulled out her cell and called her driver to pick her up at one of her favorite boutiques. Then she continued on, sticking to the crowd, hoping she'd blend in. So no one would notice the fake woman crying real tears.

~ ~ ~

Jake was pissed off. They'd had a great day together for the second time and now Jenny, or whoever she was, had given him some bullshit excuse. He was starting to suspect she wasn't who she said she was. Things didn't add up. Why she had no digital footprint for starters. He hadn't imagined the very real tenderness in her expression when he gave her the gentleman treatment, or the easy way they were together, or the lust in her eyes whenever they got close. Why couldn't she just be straight with him? Was she a fugitive? Witness protection program? What?

He couldn't shake his foul mood the whole way back from the city. He didn't even consider flying back home. He needed to talk to Josh.

As soon as he reached Josh's place, he took one step inside, and Josh called from the sofa, "That bad, huh?"

Jake flopped down next to him. "She dumped me."

Josh turned the volume down on the game. "Sorry."

Jake grunted.

"Did you tell her who you were?"

"No."

"Maybe it would make a difference. Tell her what you can offer her. Ya know, the jet, the yacht, the villa in France. Candy to a baby."

Jake blew out a breath. "I don't want her to want me for that. I want her to want me for me."

Josh raised a brow in unspoken twin speak. *She doesn't.*

Jake shoved a hand through his hair. "Something's weird about her. I can't put my finger on it."

Josh went to the kitchen. "You want something?"

"Nah." He grabbed the remote and turned up the volume.

Josh returned a few minutes later with a plate of reheated meatloaf and mashed potatoes. He ate pretty good from takeout at Garner's. They watched the game in silence until a commercial came on and Josh nudged him. "Hey, I got something that'll get your mind off weird Jenny."

"I didn't say she was weird. Just something weird about her."

Josh shoved some meatloaf in his mouth and chewed before saying, "Ty told me he's doing motorcycle stunts in the movie *Fierce Longing*. He's stoked. The other guy got injured and they called him in last minute. Anyway, they're filming not far from here. You know the Fierce trilogy? Mad's really into it."

"Yeah, I've heard some women talking about it."

"Guess who's in it."

Jake let out a breath. "I don't know. Just tell me." He didn't keep up with celebrity gossip.

"Claire Jordan." Josh slowly shook his head, a goofy smile on his face. "She is smoking. Did you see her in *Neighborly Attraction* or *Pleasant Town*?"

"Sound like chick flicks." He stared at his brother. "You watch that shit?"

"*Blue Haze*?"

His mind flashed to a killer bod streaked with dirt. "That spiked bikini? Hell. That was hot." It was a post-apocalyptic movie and she'd played a reckless gang leader in a steamy desertlike future where everyone wore rags and metal. That bikini was something. He didn't remember a single thing she said in the movie. It was all about the way she moved.

"Ty invited me for lunch on Tuesday," Josh said. "It's a closed set, but we can meet him at craft services. You want to go? Maybe you'll get to meet Claire Jordan and be like Jenny who?"

Yeah. He wished he could forget Jenny that easily.

But what else was he going to do? Mope around, pining for Jenny. "Sure."

Josh finished his dinner and texted Ty, who got them on the security list.

That gave Jake the whole next day to work remotely and try not to think about Jenny. He was dealing with the latest crisis with their proprietary technology on the black market in Tanzania, which should've kept him focused, but his mind kept drifting to the puzzle of Jenny. He started thinking maybe she was married. Maybe she had a different last name. Maybe she used to be a man. All kinds of crazy shit came to him. But he knew she was all woman. It had been dark, but everything had been in the right place, and her responses were pure feminine bliss. Dammit. She was driving him nuts.

The next day they showed up at noon and were shown to an outdoor eating area with a couple of long tables tucked under some white tents. A palatial stone mansion sat in the distance, surrounded by acres of manicured lawn. A marble fountain in the center of a circular driveway added to the old European feel. Cool place to film.

Ty met them as soon as they cleared the security gate, striding toward them in a black leather jacket and jeans. "You made it!" Ty exclaimed, giving them both a hug with a lot of pounding on the back. "Not easy to find this place in the sticks."

Josh grinned. "I've got an internal GPS. Anything good for lunch?"

"Yeah, we got sandwiches and meatball subs," Ty said. "Come on."

They headed to the tents where the crew was eating. He and Josh helped themselves to meatball sandwiches. They always preferred hot food to cold.

They settled at the table with Ty, who introduced them to some of the crew—camera guys, lighting, sound, and a couple of people from wardrobe.

Josh leaned across the table to Ty and whispered, "Will we meet Claire Jordan? Or Blake?"

Ty shook his head. "Nah. They don't eat at this craft services. They have gourmet meals brought in for the upper level. We're second tier."

Jake raised a brow. Sounded snooty. Too big to eat with the little people.

They were halfway through lunch when a hush fell over the group.

Ty whispered, "Claire Jordan."

Jake looked up to see *the* Claire Jordan standing at the other end of the table, talking to some of the crew. A large man hovered nearby, probably a bodyguard. She was smoking hot in a white leather jacket, navy skirt, and matching heels. Dark brown hair fell to her shoulders. She was made up, but not overly so, her

skin flawless and glowing. Probably her costume for
the movie. He'd read a little about the movie on the
way here. She played a librarian that tangled with a
billionaire tycoon in a dangerous game of corporate
espionage. He knew he was staring, but he couldn't
help it. There was something about her, something so
familiar. He'd only seen her in that bikini movie and
his focus hadn't been on her face. She looked
completely different as a librarian. Her gaze caught on
his briefly, and all of his senses heightened, goose
bumps on top of goose bumps, a visceral response to
the flash of recognition that shot through his brain. He
did know her. He knew those eyes, the cheekbones,
the straight nose, those full sweet lips. This was Jenny.
His Jenny. It had to be. Or Jenny had an identical
twin. Shit. Twins switching with twins? Unlikely. It
had to be her.

She turned back to the camera guys, speaking
quietly. He rubbed the goose bumps on his arms. He
couldn't tear his gaze away, his pulse pounding in his
ears. The camera guys were very respectful, listening
and nodding to whatever she was saying. He couldn't
hear her from this far away, especially with Ty and
Josh trash-talking about the last basketball game.

Claire shifted, crossing toward the center of the
group and addressing everyone with a small smile.
"How're you all doing? Enjoying this beautiful day?"

His pulse spiked with adrenaline. He knew that throaty, husky voice. The coloring was different—brown hair, hazel eyes—but that face, that body, that voice. How could this be? Why would Hailey set up Josh with the famous Claire Jordan? What did Claire Jordan want with a bartender? This was why she couldn't see him anymore. She wasn't a fugitive or married or a man. It was much worse than any of that (maybe not the man thing)—she was too big a star for a lowly bartender.

He stared at her, willing her to make eye contact, needing to see recognition in her eyes. She finally did and froze, jaw agape, looking first from him and then to Josh sitting next to him. He hadn't told her one of his brothers was his identical twin. She quickly turned away. She definitely recognized him, though he wasn't sure she knew which one was Josh and which was him. Not many people could tell them apart on first meeting.

"Claire!" Ty called. "My brothers wanted to meet you."

She turned back, her expression composed into a smile that seemed forced. "Of course." She came over and stood next to Ty.

"This is Josh and Jake. Identical, obviously. You can tell them apart, though. Josh smiles more and dresses like a slob." Ty pointed at Josh.

Josh grinned.

Jake couldn't speak, still in shock. He couldn't believe he'd been so hung up on a person that didn't exist. Was any of what they had real?

"Nice to meet you both," Claire said with a cheery wave, already backing away. She whirled and strode back to the mansion.

Jake bided his time, waiting for everyone to finish lunch and head back to work. Then he pulled Josh aside. Ty followed them; he wasn't needed on set for another hour. "Claire is Jenny," Jake said in a low tone.

"Be serious," Josh said.

Jake gave him the silent twin look.

Josh's eyes widened. "Holy shit! Why would she want Hailey to set her up on a blind date?"

"I don't know why she did it, but it was her." He did a quick rewind through his time with Jenny. How they'd made love in the dark, how she'd told him not to mark her neck or touch her hair. Probably because she couldn't play a shy librarian with a love bite on her neck. And that red hair must've been a wig. Fucking A. He felt like an idiot. He'd wanted her so bad he hadn't even questioned her requests. The moment she said he could do anything he wanted besides biting or hair touching, he dove in. And he didn't even get to do everything he wanted. Now he never would. She was so far out of his league.

Ty stared, disbelieving. "This Claire? The sexiest woman alive? You did *not* go out with Claire Jordan."

"He slept with her," Josh said.

They both gave him impressed looks.

"I can't believe I didn't put it together right away," Jake said. "Her hair and eye color were different when I was with her, red hair and the greenest eyes I've ever seen." He smacked his forehead. Contacts. How could he not have realized it? He stared at the mansion, where pseudo Jenny was filming the biggest movie of the year.

He rubbed the back of his neck. Where did this leave him? He thought back to their easy conversation, the chemistry, the passion. That couldn't be faked. Even if Jenny wasn't real, and even though he wasn't Josh, the connection was real. He had a momentary worry over the sexiest-woman-alive label, but then he remembered he was the sexiest bachelor in Silicon Valley. That should count for something! His natural confidence returned. Hell, she said he was awesome in bed. Of course, she thought he was Josh at the time but whatever. He *was* awesome in bed and he could be more awesome given the chance.

He turned to Ty. "Can you pass along a message for me?"

"To Claire Jordan?" Ty croaked.

"Yeah."

"Come on," Ty moaned. "She's my boss. Not just lead actress. This is under her production company. If I piss her off, she's going to fire me. This is a big movie. I'm only here on her good graces as a last minute substitute."

"I'll owe you," Jake said. "Whatever you want."

Ty considered that. He knew Jake could come through with some pretty spectacular stuff.

Jake went on. "Just tell her Josh knows who went on that date."

Ty's brows slammed together. "Josh? I thought you went out with her."

"We switched places for the night," Jake said. "Josh wanted to mess with this other girl."

Ty shook his head at the two of them. "You guys are *fucked up*. I can't believe you're still pulling this twin shit."

"Just pass along the message," Jake barked. "I'll straighten out the Josh thing once I talk to her again."

"Fine." Ty jabbed a finger at him. "But you owe me big time, and I *will* call it in."

"Anything," Jake said and meant it.

Ty grinned. "I could use a new Ducati. There's this sweet honey of a bike." That was a top-of-the-line motorcycle. At least that was probably what Ty wanted. The best.

"Done."

Josh piped up. "So what do I get for making this all possible?"

"You get to tweak Hailey's nose," Jake replied. "It's what you live for, isn't it?"

Josh shoved Jake's shoulder. Hard. He shoved him back.

"Later," Ty said and jogged back to work.

"Tell me how it goes," Jake called.

Ty raised a hand in acknowledgment and kept going.

Josh turned to him. "You really think you have a shot with Claire Jordan?"

She was so far out of his league it wasn't even funny. But he did have hope because she obviously wanted a taste of something different than the usual Hollywood elite. And he could hold his own with the rich and famous. "Yeah, I do."

Josh shook his head. "Damn, I wish I'd gone on that date."

Jake palmed Josh's face and shoved. "With this face?"

Josh slapped his hand away. "What was I thinking?" he said with a laugh.

"Besides, then you would've missed the chance to go out with Hailey."

"I go out with her all the time." He put on a bored

expression that didn't fool Jake for a minute. "Wedding after wedding after wedding. I wouldn't go if she didn't pay me."

"Sure, sure."

"Shut up."

They headed toward the access road where Josh had parked.

"Don't forget your business dinner with the lovely lady," Jake said just to razz him. "Not just weddings."

"I'm not into her," Josh insisted. "I tolerate her. That's all."

Jake shot him a skeptical look.

Josh smirked. "Damn, I can't believe you got Claire Jordan for a blind date. All I ever get is the walking wounded."

"Your own fault."

"You gonna stick around a while?"

"Hell yeah. I'm just getting started."

Josh rubbed his hands together. "This is gonna be good."

CHAPTER NINE

Claire returned to the set, trying to focus on what needed to be done for the next scene, but she was freaking out. She never expected to run into Josh here. Double shock he had an identical twin. It was so bizarre to see not one but two Joshs that she nearly yelped in surprise. Only the presence of the crew made her keep it together. She wasn't sure if he recognized her. Both men had stared at her, but most men did the first time they met her. They either had a tough-girl *Blue Haze* bikini fantasy or a virginal *Neighborly Attraction* fantasy, neither of which was her. She blew out a breath. Back to work. She put on her headset and called for the key players to report to the dining room.

A short while later, everyone was in place, and she did a quick rundown of the dinner scene with Blake and the crew. The prop master, Diane, wasn't happy with the look of the fruit bowl and they waited while she refreshed some fruit from the kitchen.

Blake turned to go. He preferred to lounge in his trailer if he wasn't on camera.

"Stay close by," she told Blake. "We need to get started as soon as props are in place."

Blake crossed his arms and stared at the dining room, jaw tight.

"It won't be long," she assured him.

He made a sour face, but said nothing. He didn't have to, he communicated enough nonverbally to let everyone know how he felt. Lately, he'd been giving her more attitude. She'd heard his own fledgling production company wasn't doing well. He couldn't get investors in the films he wanted to produce. It was a tricky thing to do, requiring finesse and marketing savvy. Claire had produced her first film out of pocket. The success of that had given investors confidence in backing her future films. Except the Fierce trilogy, she'd gone all in on that deal because she knew it could be big and she wanted it all to herself, answering to no one. She'd mentioned to Blake that he should consider investing his own money when they'd first talked about his new venture six months ago, but he'd refused to even consider investing in himself. He said his name should be enough for people to open their wallets.

Ty approached, a bulkier inked version of Josh.

Now that she'd seen the brothers together, all she could see was Josh when she looked at Ty. The deep brown eyes, the angle of his cheekbones, the athletic grace of his body. She'd spent the morning with Ty yesterday when she'd supervised the exterior shots of Damon tearing it up on his motorcycle. For some reason, her knees locked, bracing for bad news.

Relax, she told herself. He probably wanted to ask her a question. After the dinner scene, Damon, played by Ty for the stunt, would take off on his bike in a fury and spin out on the edge of the circular driveway.

She turned and pasted on a smile.

Ty smiled back. "Hey, Claire, thanks for meeting my brothers. It meant a lot to them."

"Of course."

Blake looked over and raised a brow. "I thought this was a closed set."

"Crew can meet off set for lunch if their guest gets security clearance," Claire replied. Craft services was far enough away from filming to keep a closed set, and she'd learned that a happy crew always made filming easier. Over the last three films, hiring many of the same crew, they'd developed a level of trust. No one had taken advantage of the privilege. Most of the time, there were no guests.

"I'll be you out there on the bike," Ty told Blake. "Stunt double."

"Make me look good," Blake said.

Ty grinned and raised his palms like it was a given. He turned to Claire, gave her a pointed look, and said, "Josh knows who went on that date."

Her stomach dropped. Shit. He knew it was her. It was only a matter of time before he sold the story to the highest bidder. Claire Jordan in disguise. Claire Jordan drunk in the woods. Claire Jordan in a seedy one-night stand. Or, worse, Claire and Blake on the rocks, what did this mean for Damon and Mia? Her movie would be sunk. The buzz on Damon and Mia killed. She swallowed down the bile in her throat.

"Who's Josh?" Blake asked.

Ty slipped away.

Blake was saying something to her, but her hearing dimmed as a ringing went through her ears. She stumbled to a dining room chair and sat down. Sweat broke out on her upper lip. She dropped her head in her hands, dizzy and hoping she didn't pass out. She heard a commotion and the next thing she knew her assistant was insisting she drink a glass of water.

She lifted her head to find everyone staring at her with a look of concern. Except Blake, who almost looked pleased, like he wanted to see her taken down a peg. It was that smirking look on Blake's face that made her pull it together.

"I'm fine," she said. "I skipped lunch and got a

little light-headed. Won't make that mistake again."
She often ate alone in her trailer, so no one would
doubt her white lie. She took in the fruit bowl. "Looks
like we're all set. Diane, thanks for your keen eye. Let's
get back to work."

She took a drink of water, and before she could set
it down, her assistant whisked it away. She stood,
stronger now and focused. No one could put her off
her game. She'd deal with Josh later.

Unfortunately, it wasn't that easy. She was on edge
the rest of the day, which she funneled into the
emotional scene between her and Damon where
Damon suspects Mia of having a secret, of possibly
betraying him. Yeah, she knew a little about that,
though she feared Josh would be the one betraying her.

On a brief break, she texted Hailey to arrange a
meeting with Josh. She needed to talk to him face-to-
face and find out exactly what he planned to do with
this information. She told Hailey to send him to the
private lounge where the book club met. No way was
she inviting him to her suite. Because while she'd been
pretending as Jenny, there was no doubt that the
chemistry they had was very real. The last thing she
needed was to fall into bed with him a second time as
herself. She'd only be getting herself in deeper,
exposing much more than she could risk.

Her life was becoming the kind of melodrama she

acted out on the big screen.

She wasn't at all surprised to hear back a short while later that Josh was willing to meet. Anyone in his position would. He'd probably walk in with his hand out. She wasn't averse to paying him not to talk. It would save her a lot of headache in the long run. Things would get stickier if he had photos. She hadn't seen him take pictures, but who knew what he had done when she was sleeping. It had happened before.

Finally the appointed time arrived. She stepped into the lounge, took a seat at the long table, and waited. She wanted a table between them. This was a negotiation and she would do better with some distance. Her bodyguard had instructions, along with a photo provided by Hailey, to escort him in. Hailey had texted her a few times, apologizing profusely for the date gone wrong, but she didn't blame her. It was her own silly longing to feel normal again. That wasn't who she was anymore.

The door opened, Frank poked his head in to give her a heads-up, and then let Josh in. She watched him approach in a crisp white button-down shirt, gray dress pants, and leather shoes. His stride was purposeful and confident. For a brief moment she had a sense they were having a business meeting. Something was different about him. Not just the dressier clothes. An attitude. The way he held himself.

Fury rose up in her. She'd been played. He'd been calculating how to get the most out of his time with her. He must've known who she was all along. She'd suspected he knew something at their last meeting. Who told? Did one of her new friends betray her? Mad? Hailey? She didn't want that to be true. Maybe he'd recognized her. She really hoped that was it.

He stopped on the other side of the table, directly across from her, and stared. "I can't believe it was really you. I'm still in shock."

"Like you didn't know."

"I didn't know. Not until I saw you at lunch today." He kept staring. "Your hair and eyes were so different, and you acted almost shy as Jenny. You're not shy at all, are you?"

"No." And now she felt a little paranoid. She'd been about to dump her new friends over an imagined betrayal. She rubbed her forehead. "Please, have a seat."

He pulled out a chair and took a seat, his eyes never leaving hers. "Your eyes were so green. Contacts, right?"

"Yes."

"Why?"

She ignored the question. She couldn't give him any more ammunition. Not until she knew what he'd do with what he already knew. She steepled her hands on the table, keeping a carefully neutral expression. "So now you know I'm Jenny. What do you plan to do with this information?"

"Why did you do it?" He studied her, searching her expression. It reminded her of how warm he'd been—smiling at her, talking, playing around, kissing her.

She stifled a sigh. That time was over. "What does it matter?"

"Is this why you couldn't see me anymore? Because you're famous?"

"Yes."

He frowned, a deep V forming between his brows. "Because I'm a nobody bartender. You think you're above that."

Her hackles rose. She was as down-to-earth as anyone when you got to know her. It was just that she had to keep her social circle small, by necessity. "Of course not."

"Sounds exactly like that to me." He spread his arms wide across the backs of the chairs next to him and leaned back insolently in his seat. "Claire Jordan is too big for the little people."

"Don't put words in my mouth," she snapped. She told herself to calm down, not to give him any more dirt for the whopper of a story he already had, but it was extremely difficult, especially now when he was smirking at her.

He dropped his arms from the chairs and slowly leaned forward, a challenge in those deep brown eyes. "Then explain it in your own words."

"I don't have to explain anything to you."

"Then what am I doing here?" he asked in an arrogant tone. Like he knew he had her in a vulnerable position.

She wanted to squeeze him by the throat. She couldn't believe this was the same warm charming gentleman bartender she'd been thinking longingly of, wishing she could see him for a third date and a fourth and *augh*. She had a quick internal battle between ordering him out or proceeding as rationally as possible. Then he spoke again, arrogant as all hell, and rational took a hike.

"Again, I ask you, *Claire Jordan*, what am I doing here?"

"Get out," she spat, too irritated for any kind of negotiating.

He leaned back in his seat. "No."

She leapt to her feet. "No? I'll have you kicked out of here the moment I raise my voice. Frank will—"

"Sit down."

"Who the hell—"

"Come on," he said in a bored tone like *she* was the one wasting *his* time. "You got me all the way here to your supersecret meeting spot. What do you want?"

She sat abruptly, stunned that he was asking what she wanted. This whole thing was about what he wanted from her. "What do *I* want?"

"Yeah."

"I want to know what you plan to do with this information. I want to know if you have pictures."

He looked at her like she was nuts. "Pictures? Did you see me taking pictures?"

"Maybe when I was sleeping."

"I slept like the dead after you had your way with me. *Three* wicked times. Maybe you're the one with pictures."

She snort-laughed, surprising herself. "First of all, no. Second of all, who would want them?"

He crossed his arms. "Maybe you would."

She got serious. "Don't turn this around on me. I'm the one at risk here. Did you talk to anyone? Did you tell the press?"

He raised a brow. "Tell them what?"

He wasn't as sharp as she'd thought. This could be to her advantage. "Well, maybe we could arrange…" She trailed off as his gaze turned warm and tender.

He stood, walking around the table to her, and she fought to remain calm, but the closer he got, the more her pulse spiked, sending a surge of raw desire coursing through her.

He stopped next to her chair, reached out and cradled her face in one hand. Her breath caught. He slowly leaned down, close, so close, his lips a breath away. She couldn't move. She didn't want to move.

He shifted near her ear. "Am I not supposed to share how much I liked Jenny?"

Her heart leapt to her throat. "I'm sorry," she whispered.

He dropped his hand and leaned against the table next to her, considering her for a long moment. She didn't know what to say. Guilt swamped her.

He slowly shook his head. "Why pretend? You could have anyone."

She met his eyes and gave him the truth. She owed him that much. "I guess I just missed feeling normal."

"I missed the sweet girl-next-door type."

"Like you thought I was," she said softly.

"Is any part of you like Jenny? Or was the whole thing an act?"

"Josh, before I say anything else, I need to know if you're going to tell the press about this. About Jenny."

He stared at her for a long moment like he was thinking hard.

"I'll pay you to keep it secret," she rushed on. "I can get you five thousand cash within the hour. Think what that could do for you. That's a lot of money." And she'd paid a lot more than that on similar occasions.

He straightened. "You're something, Claire Jordan." She hated the way he kept saying her full name. Like he was reminding her she'd wronged him. "You think I couldn't get more than that from some celebrity rag?"

She'd underestimated him. "Name your price. But I want it in writing that you won't share any information on me, Jenny, or any of our time together. I have a nondisclosure in my purse." She reached for it.

"Don't bother," he said with a look of disgust. "I have no interest in telling anyone about you, and I sure as hell don't want your money."

She instantly regretted bringing up the money. He'd told her how much he liked Jenny. He must be so upset to know Jenny wasn't real. "Josh, I—"

He turned and strode toward the door, his long legs eating up the distance. She didn't remember him ever moving so fast before.

She stood. "Wait!"

He stopped, and then his shoulders dropped like he'd let out a big sigh. Or maybe he was dreading whatever she was about to say. What was she going to say? Another apology? Sorry for messing with your head and stabbing you in the heart?

He slowly turned, gazing at her silently across the

room, waiting.

Some unknown force had her moving toward him before she realized what she was doing. She stopped directly in front of him. Up close, his dark eyes were conflicted, angry and also sad. It was the sadness, the hurt she'd caused, that made her blurt the truth. "I wish I could be her for you. I never thought one fun date, well, two actually, would get so complicated."

He looked over her shoulder. "Yeah, complicated."

"It's too hard to date a civilian. The hours, the constant travel. It's hard to keep relationships going like that. You need a small-town girl. Like you thought I was."

His lips formed a grim line. Finally he held out his hand. "I guess this is goodbye."

She shook his hand, the warmth of it bringing a tingling rush. Her eyes met his in an electric connection, the urge to throw herself in his arms overwhelming.

But then he stepped back. "Goodbye, Jenny."

He was saying goodbye to the fake woman, not her. It didn't make her feel any better because she'd brought a lot of herself to Jenny, but there was too much Claire Jordan in the way for that to matter.

She crossed her arms, hugging herself. She hated goodbyes. Her whole life seemed like one long goodbye to people and places. First because of her dad's military career, then moving from movie set to set all over the world.

He stood in front of her, waiting for her to say goodbye, but she couldn't do it.

"We had fun that night, didn't we?" she asked. "And on the boat."

His expression was solemn. "Yeah, we did."

He turned and left without a backward glance.

She nearly collapsed from the awful guilt and longing. "Goodbye, Josh," she said to the empty room.

She dashed at an errant tear, squared her shoulders, and went out the back entrance to her private suite. Alone again with her silent shadow trailing close by.

CHAPTER TEN

Hailey was in her glory. The women were bonding, giddy with excitement as they got their hair done together at her favorite local salon Looking Styling, though now that she thought about it, Armand should try Hair Cuts With Happy Endings. She was bringing him a lot of wedding business, and now the Happy Endings Book Club. Later today they'd show up on Claire's set and play extras in the corporate party scene. Hollywood, here we come!

"Sorry, Hails," Armand said when she suggested the new name. "You're Happy Endings, and I'm Styling. You can post another flyer with your new club name by the front desk if you want."

"Okay, I will." She knew better than to piss off her hairdresser. They had a sacred bond. No one touched her hair except Armand.

There were three salon chairs for hair and three more chairs in the back for manicures. Everyone was rotating through. Even Mad, who looked peeved that she had rollers in her short hair.

"You're going to look so cute," Hailey called to Mad.

Mad glared at her.

Hailey smiled over at Julia getting her nails done. She wouldn't be joining them in the extras scene. She just wanted to visit the set.

Hailey found herself thinking about that business dinner with Jake again. It bugged her how much she thought about the end of that date. One hot gaze didn't make up for the fact that he was a boring braggart. Okay, he smelled good, but any guy wearing that aftershave would've smelled good. And she'd felt nothing when she saw him at basketball. Weird how chemistry worked—on, off. So fickle. She knew from her professional matchmaking skills that it took far more than simple chemistry to get a relationship off the ground and build it into something special. Just look at Julia and Angelo. They had palpable chemistry, but it was their solid friendship that would help them go the distance. It seemed you really couldn't have one without the other for a long-lasting relationship. Of course, that made her think of Mad and her guy friends. She wondered if any of the other book club ladies had guy friends. If they did, she'd encourage them to explore if there was more there. Friends to lovers seemed to be the way to go.

Armand finished the blow-dry. Her hair fell in artful layers with a nice wave at the ends. He took the black smock off and looked at her in the mirror. "Gorgeous," he declared, admiring his work. Hailey smiled, agreeing one hundred percent with his magical styling skills.

"Thanks, Armand!" Hailey said, standing and giving him an air kiss near his silver hoop earring. His own hair, dark brown with blond highlights, was perfectly tousled in a carefully careless style. He understood about not mussing hair and makeup on important occasions.

She made the rounds, checking on her friends in various stages of highlights, blow-dry, and nails. She stopped by Charlotte first, who was getting some auburn highlights in her long dark brown hair. "You have any guy friends?" Hailey asked.

Charlotte raised a perfectly shaped brow. "Nope. No woman does."

"Of course they do. Julia and Angelo were friends. Me and Josh are friends."

"Nope," Charlotte said. "If a guy wants to be your friend, it's only because he's getting warmed up for the next step."

Hailey huffed. "That is definitely not true."

She went over to Julia, getting her nails polished

sangria red. "You and Angelo were good friends long before you got together, right? Charlotte says guys never want to be just friends. That's not true, right?"

Julia flashed a smile. "Angel and I wanted each other from day one, even if we didn't act on it." At Hailey's frown, Julia went on. "But I'm sure there are some people capable of a platonic relationship."

Hailey nodded vigorously. She turned to the group. "Anyone here have a guy friend?"

All of the women said no, except Mad, who said, "Tons. I like guys better than girls." She looked around sheepishly. "Except you guys."

Some of the women laughed; some grumbled.

"What're you thinking in that pretty head of yours?" Armand asked Hailey from where he was now supervising the highlights in Charlotte's hair. "You looking for a new way to set up your girls? Friends to lovers?"

"Hush," she said. Armand was always one step ahead of her.

"Just have a party," Armand said. "Good music, good food, drinks, they'll do the rest."

"Maybe I will," Hailey said. She worried her lower lip. But where was she going to find at least six single men to bring to a party?

Duh. Mad. She crossed to where Mad was getting the rollers out of her hair. She looked cute, the springy curls popping up all over her head like a woman from the fifties. All she needed was a cute kerchief or headband to complete the look. Maybe a sparkly butterfly barrette.

"So cute!" Hailey exclaimed.

Mad pouted. "I look like I stuck my finger in the socket."

Tara, her stylist, looked miffed. "I'm not done yet."

"Oh," Mad said. "That's good."

Tara went to work with a blow-dryer, bringing more body to Mad's hair. Hailey watched as Mad transformed from tough and spiky to soft and feminine. With the right makeup, and if Mad would stop curling her lip—

"What?" Mad barked, making Hailey jump. "Why are you just standing there? Don't you have makeup to put on or something?"

Hailey smiled, all teeth, from her pageant training. As soon as Tara switched from the hair dryer to conditioning mousse, Hailey got right to the point.

"How many guy friends do you have? Besides the guys I met at basketball." Mad had already informed her those guys weren't the marrying type.

Mad quirked her lips to the side, looking at the ceiling. "I dunno. I never counted."

"There's that many?" Hailey asked, new hope for

her wedding planning business blooming. So many love matches! All of her friends would find their happy-ever-afters!

Mad listed them all. "The basketball crew, the guys I play softball with, the guys at the dojo. Twenty, twenty-five guys."

"You have twenty-five guy friends?" Hailey exclaimed in a near shout.

"It's no big. Just guys I hang with. We're not telling each other deep dark secrets. We just do stuff together."

"Have you ever…"

"What?"

Hailey lowered her voice. "You know, dated any of them?"

Tara stopped doing Mad's hair and quirked a brow.

Mad flushed. "I told you, it's not like that. We hang out."

"You like?" Tara asked, gesturing for Mad to look in the mirror.

Mad stared at herself for a long moment before finally saying, "Doesn't look like me but whatever."

"It looks like your best you," Hailey said. "We're doing makeup for her too," she told Tara.

Mad frowned.

"Can I ask you a question?" Hailey asked while

Tara pulled out the makeup case.

"What?" Mad asked.

"With any of those guy friends, did you ever feel—"

"No!" Mad snapped. She raised her voice above the din of the salon. "Can someone take Hailey? She won't stop bugging me about my guy friends."

Hailey huffed. "Really, Mad, your manners could use work."

"We can't all be beauty queens."

"You'd never make it at a pageant," Hailey muttered.

"Ooh, burn," Mad said, shaking her fingers and blowing on them like she was cooling them off.

Hailey made the rounds, quietly inquiring on the male friend situation, only to find, disappointingly, that Mad was the only one with any guy friends at all. She had high hopes for her Happy Endings Book Club friends. Not just for business purposes. She was a romantic, and she wanted someone princely to sweep them off their feet. But where to find a prince?

After they finished with hair, makeup, and nails, they hopped in a waiting limo to a soundstage in Queens where the corporate party was being filmed. Ever since she'd become friends with Claire, she'd had numerous limo rides. It still didn't get old. She felt giddy and excited every time. There was even champagne chilling for them.

"Yes!" Mad said. "I could use a drink to take the edge off. That salon was stressful."

Hailey found salons relaxing. Someone else doing all the work of making her pretty while she just lounged in a chair. Mad looked gorgeous. She'd never realized how delicate her features were until she wore her hair like that, the soft halo of loose curls framed delicate cheekbones, doe-brown eyes, a small upturned nose, and cute little chin. She wore a black pants suit, though Hailey had tried to lend her a dress. Hailey had wanted to do a full head-to-toe shopping trip when she'd heard about the sad state of Mad's wardrobe, but Mad had shut that down with a quick, "Nah. Pants suit is fine."

"It was worth the effort," Hailey told Mad. "You look gorgeous."

"Get out," Mad said, blushing furiously. "It's smoke and mirrors."

"You are beautiful," Julia said. Everyone piled on the compliments for Mad.

"Shut up, bitches," Mad said. "I know you're just fishing for a return compliment and you won't get it out of me. You all look damn ugly."

A shocked silence fell.

"Uh, I meant that affectionately," Mad said. She turned to Hailey. "That's how I talk to my friends. Guys know it's meant as a compliment. You insult each other and call each other names."

"Women say nice things like you look beautiful," Hailey instructed patiently.

Mad rolled her eyes and sighed heavily. "Fine. You all look beautiful too." She turned to Hailey. "Now why do women say that to each other? Don't you want a guy to say that? It's not like I'm going to be your date or something." She shuddered.

"Not like I want you as my date," Hailey returned.

The women laughed. Hailey found herself laughing too. The idea of her and Mad as a couple was ridiculous. Like an evening gown with high-top athletic shoes. It just didn't go!

When they got on set, they were quickly ushered back to the green room, where they waited with bottled water and a couple of closed-circuit televisions showing the soundstage.

"Wait here," a guy with a headset said. "Claire wants to greet you personally."

They waited, giddy, and a little buzzed from champagne. Claire had provided the drink so she must've wanted them in a festive mood for the party scene. Of course she'd only provided one bottle for the seven of them so she didn't want them smashed.

"See you out there," Julia said, slipping out of the room. She was the only one with complete access to every part of the set. Claire had made her a producer.

They waited around for a while, and just when they were getting restless and bored, the guy with the headset came in and called them to set. Hailey was surprised to see the set wasn't as large as she'd thought it would be. Three white walls, some strategically placed round tables with white tablecloths, a dance floor, and a buffet area. Potted plants in two of the corners. There were three cameras and numerous lights hanging from a metal grid overhead.

Julia gestured them over to where she was standing with a group of people dressed in suits and cocktail dresses. Maybe they were extras too. Hailey immediately recognized Julia's husband, Angelo, and rushed over to greet him, giving him a hug.

"Are you going to be in the scene today?" Hailey asked.

Angelo shook his head. "Nope. Just here to watch. Julia and I are keeping a low profile. But my brothers are here with their wives." He gestured to where two stunning dark-haired Italian men stood with three equally gorgeous men with light brown hair.

Hailey did a quick count of the women standing with them. "All of them married?"

"Yup," Angelo said with a smile.

"Damn."

Claire swooped in. "Hey, girls! Looking good."

The women all gathered around Claire, thanking

her for including them.

"Is that Blake?" Charlotte whispered, looking over at a tall dark-haired man getting his makeup touched up.

"That's him," Claire confirmed.

"Omigosh," Ally said, fanning herself. She was prone to exuberance. "He's even hotter in person!"

"How can you tell that from across the room?" Mad asked.

"He is," Charlotte breathed.

"Can we meet him?" Hailey asked.

Claire gave them an indulgent look. "Of course I'd love to introduce you, but, ladies, you do not want him for real life. He won't even talk to you if he doesn't think he has a chance of getting in your pants."

"But he can," Ally breathed.

The other women agreed.

"We'll be on our best behavior," Hailey said.

Claire gestured for them to follow, and they moved eagerly, but with much sophistication, over to meet Mr. Blake Grenier in the flesh.

"Hey, Blake," Claire said. "These are my friends. They'll be extras in the party scene today. This is Hailey, Mad, Charlotte, Ally, Lauren, and Carrie."

The women all gave him a flirty hello, except Mad, who jerked her chin at him and said, "Hey."

Blake scanned the group before landing on Hailey,

giving her a once-over that warmed her. *He picked me!* He crooked a finger at her, beckoning her closer, and she moved, drawn to him like a total fan girl about to lose her shit.

"You look like you've done this before," he said in a husky charming voice. His eyes were a stunning blue, his jaw masculine perfection, his lips sensuous with a hint of a smile. She bit back a swoony sigh. "What else have you been in?"

She fluttered a hand in the air. "Oh, no. I'm not an actress. This is my first time."

He gave her a panty-melting smile that was even better in real life than on the big screen. "I'll show you the ropes," he said with a wink.

She turned back to her friends, jaw dropped, silently communicating with wide eyes, *Can you believe this?*

"We gotta go." Claire pulled Hailey a distance away, calling over her shoulder, "Thanks, Blake."

Hailey pulled her elbow out of Claire's grip. "I wasn't done talking to him."

"I told you he only wants to talk to women he thinks he can sleep with. You deserve better than that."

Hailey dug her heels in. "I'm sure that's not true. He seems friendly, flirty, and nice."

"Just trust me." Claire leaned close. "He's an asshole."

Hailey looked over Claire's shoulder to where Blake was…omigod! He was smoldering at *her*, Hailey Adams! She couldn't believe Blake Grenier, star of *Neighborly Attraction*, *Pilot Games*, and *River Crush*, was an asshole. He was everything every girl dreamed of—a sexy neighbor, a charming pilot winning the war and the girl, a down-home country boy oozing sex. Not to mention a swoony billionaire from her very favorite books of all time, the Fierce trilogy. She was *not* missing this chance to get up close and personal.

She stepped around Claire and returned to Blake, who was still getting touched up by a makeup lady. It couldn't possibly be true that he wouldn't speak to her if she wasn't going to bed with him. That was ridiculous. Did that mean he only talked to one person ever? The person he was about to bang?

"I have a boyfriend," Hailey announced, a small white lie to explain (in a classy way) that she was not available for sexy times with him.

Blake raised an eyebrow. It was kind of forward, he hadn't asked if she was single, but Hailey needed to prove Claire wrong. Blake Grenier was not that kind of guy.

"But I'd love to chat with you some more," Hailey said. "Have you read the Fierce trilogy books? What made you take the role? How much do you think you're like Damon?"

Blake ignored her, instead flirting with the makeup lady.

Hailey fumed. He was an asshole. She whirled on her heel and returned to Claire and her friends.

Claire took one look at Hailey and said, "Don't take it personally. Most of the men I meet are like that."

Hailey's eyes widened. That sounded horrible. She spoke in a low whisper just for Claire's ears. "Then I'm glad I set you up with Josh."

Claire grimaced. "Yeah."

"How did it go last night now that he knows who you are?"

"I was honest and told him I couldn't see him again."

For some reason, Hailey felt more sympathetic toward Josh than Claire. It was the first time Josh had actually liked someone enough to want more than one date, and Claire left him out in the cold just because he wasn't a big movie star. So few people were big stars, really, and Josh had his good points.

A woman rushed up to Claire and whispered in her ear. Claire frowned. The woman showed her something on her cell phone. Claire flushed bright red before snapping, "Tell her I'll call her back. I'll take care of it."

The woman rushed off.

"What's wrong?" Hailey asked.

Claire pulled Hailey aside to a quiet corner of the space. "Someone talked to the press about me secretly dating Josh. The headlines are saying Damon and Mia split. It's royally fucked things for the movie. I can't believe this. He said he wouldn't say anything. My publicist is freaking out."

"I can't believe Josh would do something like that."

She scowled. "Somebody did."

"I swear it wasn't me. Or anyone from book club. We would never do that to you."

Claire rubbed her temple. "I know. I'm not blaming you. It had to be Josh. Tell him to meet me tonight, same place, same time. I need to lock this down before it gets too far."

"Of course. I'll text him right away. Don't worry about a thing. I'm sure no permanent damage was done." At Claire's shiny eyes, Hailey rushed on. "This is fixable, and I'll do whatever I can to help with your good publicity efforts. Just say the word."

Claire shook her head. "I've got the best publicist in the business, and a lawyer if it comes to that. Just get Josh to show tonight."

"On it." Hailey texted Josh. She knew she wouldn't hear back immediately. He usually worked afternoon to evening and wasn't glued to his cell like most people.

Claire blew out a breath. "I have to get through this scene; then I'll call my publicist. I've got another scene after that. Then Josh." She put her hands on her hips. "It's going to be a long day."

Hailey tried to hug her, but Claire quickly pulled away. Hailey felt bad for her part in this mess. She'd really thought Josh would be a nice break for Claire. She was still having trouble believing that Josh would deliberately hurt Claire. Was he that desperate for money for his dream bar? She didn't want to think that about him, she always tried to give people the benefit of the doubt, but it wasn't looking good.

Blake stopped Claire on her way back to the set and spoke quietly to her, his hand on her lower back in a close rather intimate hold. Claire nodded, put her hand on his arm, and seemed to be thanking him for something. Odd because she thought Claire didn't like him much and that Blake didn't talk to women unless he knew he had a shot with them. Hailey shook her natural love instincts off. It must be because Claire was the boss that Blake spoke to her, and, of course, all the sex scenes in the movie would naturally lead to a comfortable intimacy.

A short while later, they were ushered onto the set where Claire and Blake were acting out the scene. Hailey and the other extras were soon given their instructions—stand around, mouth pretend conversations, and occasionally toss back nonalcoholic champagne. They all started with great enthusiasm, and Hailey even threw her head back a few times in silent laughter at something Charlotte mouthed to her. Her enthusiasm didn't last long.

Claire stopped by to ask Hailey to keep it low-key. The focus should be on Damon and Mia.

Hailey worked on being low-key, which was very difficult for someone used to shining in the spotlight as she had in all those pageants. And also she was in a movie! And not just any movie. Her favorite book come to life! They had to shift groups and people several times during filming, bringing her to mingle with Angelo's older brother, Nico, who was as good looking as Blake Grenier! Maybe even better. Pure Italian hottie. If there were beauty pageants for men, he'd have a closet full of tiaras. Nico was super good at being low-key, not even moving his mouth at all. Just standing there. She kept up her animated nonconversations as she worked through Angelo's brothers and their wives, then her friends, even once at the bar in the background behind Damon.

Four hours later, her enthusiasm was flagging. Claire must've made them run through the same scene a hundred times. Hailey was so bored. And hungry too. Didn't they break for dinner or something?

By the time they finished an hour later, Hailey was so over show business. It looked a lot more glamorous on the big screen than it was in real life. She didn't know how Claire managed all the repetition. Each time they had to bring all their energy to the scene over and over and over like it was the very first time, until the take was perfect. If even one thing was off with lights, sound, the actors, wardrobe, makeup, they had to set up all over again!

Hailey drooped back to the green room where they'd left their purses. She checked her cell for a text from Josh and was relieved to see he agreed to meet Claire tonight as she'd requested. She let Claire know, who was already bossing people around to set up for the coatroom scene. Claire thanked her and went back to work. Poor Claire. Who knew how many takes that scene would require?

Mad was pumped. She snagged her canvas messenger bag and flung it over her shoulder. "I can't wait to see us in the movie. We're famous! Let's hit Garner's. First round's on me."

The women agreed heartily and made their way back to the limo, chattering about their exciting day. Hailey just felt tired. She'd probably worn herself out with full-throttle excitement from the moment she'd woke this morning at six. Now it was five thirty. She told herself to rally. What was the point in getting all glam with her besties if they didn't celebrate together?

It was nearly seven when they got to the bar. Josh was working his usual shift. He should leave soon if he wanted to be in the city for Claire's requested meeting at nine. Claire's hours might be long, but they were strictly defined by the union regulations for everyone she'd hired.

Mad slapped her hand on the bar. "Beers on me."

"I'll take chardonnay," Julia said.

"Martini," Charlotte said.

All of them changed their drink orders except Mad. Hailey remained quiet. She'd just have water. She was already tired and alcohol would likely put her to sleep. She should probably grab some dinner soon.

Josh eyed Mad. "What the hell did they do to you?"

Mad touched her hair self-consciously. "I told ya I was going to be in that movie."

Josh shook his head, poured a beer on tap and set it in front of her. "Too much makeup."

"Whatever," Mad said, sliding onto the stool next to Hailey and ratting her out. "Hailey says we're gorgeous."

Josh's eyes landed on Hailey. She felt herself flush under his scrutiny. "This all your doing?"

"No. But I was happy to help. The where and the why are top secret." They weren't supposed to talk about the movie. Once it released next year, they were free to blab as much as they wanted. She whispered in Mad's ear to remind her of that.

"It's Josh," Mad said, flapping her hand at him. "He won't tell anyone about the movie."

She was probably right, but they'd given Claire their word. A mojito appeared in front of her with a mint leaf sticking out of it. Her usual drink, which she hadn't even requested.

"Thank you," she murmured.

Josh shook a martini shaker without comment. He served that to Charlotte.

"What else can I get you beautiful ladies?" he asked, giving the other women a charming smile.

After he served them all, he busied himself stacking glasses behind the bar. It wasn't too crowded on a Wednesday night at Garner's. Hailey found herself distracted, wondering when Josh was going to leave. Claire would flip out if he didn't show. She was very worked up about this bad press.

Finally Hailey couldn't take it anymore. Josh had to leave right now or he'd be late. She hopped off the bar stool and shifted down the bar to stand directly in front of him. "Don't you think you should get going soon?"

He poured another beer on tap. "I'm on until ten."

"But you said you'd meet her at nine!"

He stilled. "Yeah. That's right. How long are you ladies going to hang out?"

"I don't know. Why does that matter?"

He went back to work, not bothering to reply.

She returned to her seat, something tickling her brain, an uneasiness that something wasn't quite right. She was a little worried for Claire's sake.

CHAPTER ELEVEN

Jake was about to head to the small airport for private planes when he got a text from Josh that Claire wanted to see him again, same place, tonight. He puzzled over that. Why? What more was there to say? She saw no future with him, that much was clear, even after he'd told her he felt something real. The conversation had been at times painful, at times almost stimulating. He sensed more fire in her than the shy Jenny had, and his own natural competitiveness liked the challenge of sparring with her. He'd toyed with the idea of telling her who he was, but he stubbornly wanted her to want him for himself, not the shine to his gold-plated name. He'd been himself on those dates, except for the gentleman thing and the few times he'd been forced to come up with a Josh-like explanation for why he went on the blind date in the first place.

Josh texted again. *We got trouble*. There was a link too.

He clicked on it to find Claire splashed across a tabloid in disguise, not the Jenny disguise, one with short black hair as she walked with a tight crowd of people around her. The headline said *Meeting with her bartender lover! Mia and Damon on the rocks!*

Weird. It was like the press didn't make a distinction between the real person and the character she played. Another text popped up from Josh.

Some reporters showed up at work. Gonna lie low for a few days as soon as my shift's done.

Shit. The press must've tracked down Josh, trying to get info out of him. His twin didn't do well with aggressive people. His combat training kicked in, making him act first, ask questions later. They all knew better than to sneak up behind him.

Sorry, I'll see what I can do, Jake texted back.

His mind kept circling back to how the press knew any of this. He hadn't said a word. Josh sure as hell wouldn't. Who else knew? Ty. But his brother wasn't a snitch. Maybe it was Claire's preemptive move to control the message. He did some searching online, but none of the articles were complimentary. They made her sound like she was too good for them, playing at being what she thought of as a regular girl. A princess among the peasants. There were even pictures supposedly of Claire as Jenny. They were of a very homely woman with the headline: "Next Oscar-winning performance?"

No way a publicist would let the message be so negative. Claire must have a leak somewhere with someone close to her, someone looking to get back at her, maybe, or just earn a little side cash.

That night he was escorted by her huge bodyguard once again through the door of the private lounge. Claire leaped up and marched toward him, the fire in her eyes igniting an animal response that he tried to tamp down. He'd liked Jenny. But this woman, coming at him fired up and crazy sexy, on top of what they had before, was giving him all kinds of wicked ideas. There were layers to her, a complexity that fascinated him, and a passionate nature that he wanted to delve into deep.

She stopped in front of him, cheeks flushed pink, hazel eyes flashing. Her white V-neck shirt exposed cleavage that he well remembered tasting. Hot and sweet. Her jeans hugged her body and those black heels needed to stay while he peeled her out of the unnecessary items. He shoved his hands in his pockets so he wouldn't touch.

"How much to shut you up?" she snapped.

He considered how to move things to where he wanted. Defuse the situation and reignite a different scenario.

She snapped her fingers in his face. "Well?"

He pushed her hand out of his face. "I told you I wouldn't say anything. Why do you assume it was me?"

She narrowed her hazel eyes suspiciously. They were pretty, green and gold with a ring of deep blue. He liked her hazel eyes better than the bright green. Her hair was shoulder length and dark brown. He liked her blonde better. He'd found a picture of her in that spiked bikini and she had short spiky blond hair in it, looking all badass. This color made her look too pale in contrast.

"Josh! Are you high? Where are you?"

He forced himself to focus. "What?"

"I said you are the only one with good motive."

"Sorry, Claire Jordan, you'll have to find someone else to blame. My word is gold." He liked to use her full name because it tickled him to know her true identity after pining over the fictional Jenny. He saw now that the name held her back. She was flipping out over some tabloid headlines. He was sure she must get that all the time. It was up to her to move out from behind that name and take a chance on him.

"Would you stop calling me Claire Jordan? It's just Claire."

"Okay, Just Claire."

She made a growling noise in the back of her throat that made him rock hard. He understood a little better how much fun Josh must have riling up Hailey. He turned away, heading toward the bar on the far side of the room, hoping there was something there to take the edge off. He wasn't so good at playing the gentleman when he wanted something. And he wanted Claire with a fierceness way beyond Jenny, which had already been damn intense. This woman had him by the balls, though she didn't know it. He'd like to keep it that way.

He headed behind the bar and found an excellent merlot. He held it up. "Wine?"

"No!" She marched over to the bar and stood on the other side from him. "We're not here to party."

He unscrewed the cork and poured himself a glass. He could hear her doing some deep breathing over there, trying to get herself under control. He'd like to get her under control too, under him. He took a sip of the wine, pretending a casualness he was far from feeling.

She slapped a hand on the bar top to get his attention. She'd never lost his attention. He was hyperaware of her, every sense tuned in, from her heaving breasts to her flushed cheeks and neck, to that throaty, husky voice that even in anger turned him on. She didn't smell like vanilla and sugar today. She smelled like roses and something distinctly Claire, a tangy spiciness. Some perfume for her role in the movie? Didn't matter. He wanted to kiss and lick and suck every inch of her.

"Yes?" he drawled. "You have my undivided attention."

She pursed her full lips, making his pants even tighter. "I heard the press was all over you today. Did they bring a lot of publicity to your bar?"

He set his glass down. "I don't even own that bar." It bugged him that Josh had to lie low on account of whoever wanted something out of Claire. "I told you it wasn't me. Do you need it in blood?"

She narrowed her eyes. "It had to be you. How much?"

"I don't need your damn money."

"It always comes down to money. How much? Ten thousand? Twenty thousand?" She crossed her arms. "That's my final offer, you greedy, lying, conniving jerk!"

Jake lost it. "Do you know who I am?" he roared.

She startled.

He jammed a hand through his hair. "No, of course you don't," he said in a low voice. He took a deep breath. "I'm Jake Campbell, CEO of Dat Cloud. I took Josh's place on the blind date because he wanted to go out with someone as me to teach her a lesson, and I wanted the sweet small-town girl date. I was sick of glamorous superficial types." He placed both palms on the bar top and leaned in to make sure she heard this next part because she was just as much to blame for this mess as he was. "I was looking for something real."

She staggered back. "We were both in disguise." She slowly shook her head. "Wait, who was Josh teaching a lesson?"

"Who do you think? Hailey. The woman he loves to bug."

"Does Hailey know?"

"No."

"She will now."

"She should know."

She stared at him for a long moment. "So I'm the glamorous superficial type you're sick of." She laughed and then she couldn't seem to stop, laughing until she was bent over with it, hugging her stomach.

"I don't see what's so damn funny."

She straightened and wiped her eyes. "You're the egocentric wealthy manwhore I was sick of."

"I'm not an egocentric manwhore." He couldn't exactly deny the wealthy part.

"You slept with me on the first date."

"So did you. Next?"

"I still think you're egocentric."

He crossed his arms. "And what makes you think that?"

She puffed out her chest and strutted in front of him. "Do you know who I am? I'm Jake fucking Campbell, CEO of Dot Cloud!"

He narrowed his eyes. "Dat Cloud." And he did *not* sound like that.

She stopped and gave him a knowing look. "That right there says I am more important than everyone around me." She gestured to nonexistent people around them.

"I don't see you turning down the lifestyle."

She lifted her chin. "Check and mate."

He blew out a breath. "Look, it wasn't me who talked to the press. Someone else ratted you out. And what's the big deal anyway? You must make headlines regularly."

"The big deal is the Fierce trilogy. The fans love stories about Mia and Damon being a real thing."

"But it's not. Wait, is it?"

"No. But it gives us a lot of free press. We need that."

"So you go out with Blake on fake dates for real press?"

She sank heavily to a bar stool. "It's not...we just show up at places together and let the press make of that what they will. I'm lucky he's already getting out ahead of the story. We're going out on Saturday to the premiere of a Broadway show and the after party. That should help. But I can't have any more stories about me sneaking around with another guy."

"I still don't see why you have to sneak around at all. Can't people differentiate between fact and fiction?"

"It's just buzz. You wouldn't understand." She chewed on her lower lip. He remembered how soft her lips were, her taste, the heat that ignited between them.

"Well, it seems you have a leak somewhere. You need to focus on that." He tapped the bar in front of her. "I have nothing to gain by telling people you went out with my brother, which you didn't even do."

She waved that away. "It's a closed set. I vetted everyone personally." She paused. "Except Ty. He was a last minute addition. And he's the one who passed along your little mystery message."

"It's not him. Who else wants to spill your secrets?"

"Everyone! That's how they make their money, selling secrets to tabloids."

"Okay. Who else knows you were Jenny?"

"Just the book club, you, and I guess your twin." She shook her head. "When I saw you both sitting there, identical, I still knew which one was you."

"How did you know?" he asked quietly. That meant something to him. That meant she saw who he really was on the inside.

She looked off in the distance dreamily. "And when you walked in here last night. Something about your walk, your attitude was different. You weren't pretending anymore."

He stepped around the bar and went to her side. "No, I wasn't. And besides a few white lies to explain why I went on a blind date, I've been myself this whole time."

She gave him a skeptical look. "No. You're definitely different now."

"Different how?"

"You're not sweet and charming. You're aggressive."

He gave her his best charming smile. "Nah. I'm still sweet and charming."

Her lips twitched. "I'm afraid not."

He raised his palms. "I was instructed to act the gentleman."

Her eyes sparkled merrily. "You're not a gentleman. That must've been hard for you."

She didn't seem to mind all that much. He couldn't resist touching her, pushing a lock of hair back behind her ear. "So you're not sweet and shy, and I'm not a gentleman. We still did okay in the bedroom."

"Okay?" She pulled away. "Neither of us is who we

were then, and I don't exactly trust you."

"Why not?"

"Because you lied about who you were."

"So did you. What else you got? Let's knock down all these barriers." He chopped at the air.

She shook her head, a reluctant smile tugging at the corners of her mouth. Yeah, she wanted him. "Because men always want to sleep with Claire Jordan, and they get a lot more mileage out of that than I do."

He bit back an inappropriate suggestion of how he'd get mileage out of riding her like a beast and went for a last-ditch attempt at the gentleman thing that had worked so well when he charmed the pants off her.

Nothing came to him.

"Why did you want a gentleman so much anyway?" he asked.

"Because I never get it."

He wasn't convinced that was really what she wanted. Someone as fiery as she was would lose interest in that kind of restrained chivalry fast. The urge to pull her into his arms, slide a hand into her hair, her *real* hair, and claim that luscious mouth made him take a step back. If he read between the lines, she was explaining very well why she'd sought out a date with gentleman Josh—every guy came on strong with her. He had to tame his natural impulse to do the same.

She leaned against the bar. "Now that I think about it, anyone who was on set when Ty passed along your message would know I was on a date with Josh." She shot him a dark look. "Thanks for that. You couldn't have gone through Hailey?"

He'd been in shock. Mooning over someone who didn't exist. And wanting her back.

He went on the offense. "How else was I going to talk to you? You wouldn't give me your number. I couldn't exactly stroll past your he-man bodyguard onto a movie set." He splayed his fingers, framing her name in the air and said with a voice dripping with sarcastic reverence, "You're *Claire Jordan*."

"Why couldn't I have gotten the real Josh?" she shouted, hands on her hips. "He was book-club approved, not you."

Oh, it is on. He stepped closer, all up in her personal space, the hell with the gentleman crap. "Why couldn't I have gotten the real Jenny?"

Her eyes flashed. "Because she was a lie!"

He got in her face. "She was everything I wanted." *Until I found you.*

Her breath was coming faster now. She licked her lips.

And that was a go. Millimeters apart, he stared at her mouth.

Her voice came out soft. "You are everything I despise."

They slammed together, mouths fused, bodies in full contact from chest to aching groin. He gripped her hair and took over the kiss, sweeping his tongue inside, her taste the spicy sweetness he remembered. He slid his other hand to cup her ass, pressing her where he needed her. But he needed so much more than that.

She pushed on his chest. He lifted his head and met her eyes, dilated and full of desire just like that first night they were together. This had always been real.

"Stop," she said in a breathy voice. "We need to stop."

He stared at her mouth. Impossible. He needed her like his next breath. His brain wasn't working well enough to coax her, but then he didn't have to.

She grabbed his head and kissed him again. That worked. He lifted her, still kissing her, and carried her to the table. He set her on the edge, pushed her legs apart, and stood between them, kissing his way down her throat while his hands slid under her shirt.

"Wait," she said, pushing his hands away. "I can't—"

He nipped her earlobe. "You can."

"Not here."

He kissed her neck and then sucked. She smacked

his shoulder frantically.

He lifted his head, dizzy with lust. "What's wrong?"

"You can't leave a mark on me. It won't work for the movie."

He stroked the rapidly beating pulse of her throat. "Okay, I remember now. No marks. Where can we go?"

"Jake," she said. He loved hearing his real name. Loved it so much he didn't notice at first she was shifting away from him.

He grabbed her by the hips and slid her back up against him. She groaned when they made contact.

"I can't do this with you," she said, leaning back on her hands like she was trying to keep them to herself.

He let go of her hips. "I never betrayed you. I wouldn't. Who else knows you went out as Jenny? Find that person and then you'll see."

She bit her lower lip. "The book club knows. But they're the best friends I have. It couldn't be them, could it? Dammit. This is why I can't have real relationships. I can't trust anyone."

"You can trust me."

She sighed. "I don't even know you."

"Get to know me."

"Jake…" She looked away.

"One date, the real deal. Jake and Claire."

She was tempted. He could tell. She didn't give him a no right away and now she was searching his face, looking for the truth. He leaned forward, brushing his lips against hers, coaxing. He pulled back and met her eyes, fully prepared to do this all night if he had to. Coaxing, charming, easing his way in. He'd thought coaxing would be too difficult with the way he wanted her, but having her pull away was much harder.

She spoke quietly. "You don't want that kind of spotlight on you. It's not pretty."

It wasn't a no.

"I want you, and whatever comes with it, I don't care." He cradled her face with both hands. "I want Claire."

She closed her eyes, and he dropped his hands to her shoulders, sliding them down the satiny smooth skin of her arms to her hands. He took her hands from behind her and pulled them forward, just holding them. She didn't pull away. He sensed she was leaning toward letting him in.

Finally she spoke, the words filling him with elation. "We'd have to keep it quiet."

Not that he wanted to keep it quiet. He just wanted to be with her so much he was willing to play the game her way. For now. He kissed her softly and spoke against her lips. "Is that a yes?"

"Yes." She shoved him away. "Now stop kissing me. One date. Jake and Claire."

"Why do I have to stop kissing you?"

"Because you want to get to know me, remember?"

"I can get to know your body first. Get reacquainted."

She laughed. "Yeah. I've heard that one before."

He figured she probably did. Everyone wanted the sexiest woman alive. He'd seen the magazine giving her that honor and her bikini body splashed everywhere. He knew that kind of attention didn't always bring out the best in people, and he realized he had to stand out from the pack.

He stepped back and helped her off the table.

"Such a gentleman," she teased.

"It's all an illusion," he replied, not bothering to hide the edge of unsatisfied lust in his voice.

"Story of my life," she said breezily. "I'll text Hailey to let you know when I'm free."

"At least give me your number now that we've established how much you lust for me." She laughed, and he grinned. "I'd like to stop going through other people." He pulled his cell from his pocket, punched in the code, and handed it over.

She typed her number in while saying, "I never give this number to anyone. Only a handful of people have it on a need-to-know basis. Can you handle that kind of responsibility?"

"What do you think?" It was an honor and, hell, he'd earned it with all his restraint.

She met his eyes, fire back in hers. "I hope so. I swear I will hunt you down—"

He cut her off with a kiss. Not a gentle one. The kind that said he'd be taking what he wanted and she'd damn well like it. She sagged against him.

When he was good and ready, he broke the kiss and snagged his cell from her limp hand. "Later, Claire Jordan."

She fought back a smile and then beamed a big one at him, stunningly beautiful in her well-kissed, hot-for-him state. "Later, Jake Campbell."

He grinned and headed out the door. Now that was more like it.

CHAPTER TWELVE

Hailey was having so much fun celebrating being in a movie with her friends that she completely lost track of time. Next thing she knew, the ladies were saying goodbye. She had to make sure Josh got to Claire on time for their meeting tonight. She grabbed her cell. Oh, shit. Nine thirty.

"Josh," she called to the other end of the bar, "why're you still here?"

"I get off at ten." He wiped down the bar top, completely oblivious to his major failure to attend to Claire and her distressing situation.

"But don't you have to meet somebody?" she asked with a significant look.

Mad elbowed her. "Who's he meeting this time?"

Hailey ignored her. "Josh?"

He tossed the rag behind the bar. "Nope."

She couldn't very well scream *you have to meet Claire Jordan and fix this mess* across the bar to him.

She walked around the bar to where he was. It was empty on this side, so she leaned forward and whispered, "You're bailing on Claire?"

He rubbed the back of his neck.

She let out a breath of exasperation. What was wrong with men? Geez. It was the least he could do. She pulled out her cell to text Claire and let her know. Oh, Claire had just texted her.

She stared at her cell phone, heart pounding against her rib cage, reading the text a second time. This couldn't be—

That would mean—

What the hell!

Claire: *It was Jake I went on a blind date with. He switched with Josh, who wanted to teach you a lesson. What did that rat do?* :(

What did he do? Only take her out to a snooty restaurant, bore her silly, and pretend to be a successful businessman! And what kind of "lesson" was he teaching her? What was his ulterior motive? To brag, brag, brag in a ridiculous attempt to make her want Jake and then do a Scooby-Doo reveal that it was really Josh, the arrogant obnoxious bane of her existence that she wanted? Wrong-o!

To fool her into thinking she was good enough to hobnob with the wealthy elite? Or just to make a fool of her? He'd probably been secretly laughing at her nervous discomfort at that super-fancy restaurant.

She looked up to find Josh staring at her intently. "How could you!" she shouted.

"What'd you do this time?" Mad called with a laugh.

They both ignored Mad.

Josh just looked at her, his soulful brown eyes meeting hers in an intense gaze. Just like when he'd fooled her with that dinner and gave her that weirdly intense look! He was reminding her! As if she needed the reminder.

She leaned forward and growled a solemn vow. "Josh Campbell, you will never date in this town again."

"Get a grip," he said.

She huffed. "You are out of my business plan forever!"

Josh rested both hands on the bar in front of her and leaned close. She fought the urge to lean back. His voice was a husky whisper that gave her an involuntary shiver. "I never wanted to be in it."

"Then why did you...what was all that...augh!" She put her palm out. "I want all my money back."

"I don't have it with me. You'll have to come back to my place."

She pursed her lips. "Uh-huh. Where I suppose it's in your bedroom."

One corner of his mouth lifted. "How'd you know?"

She jabbed a finger at him. "You just hit number one on my shit list."

"That's better than number two." He laughed.

She wanted to throw something. She wanted to leap over the bar and throttle him. But she didn't. She kept it together, not wanting to give him the satisfaction. "I will get my revenge. You won't know where or when or how, but it's coming when you least expect it."

His smile was slow and devious. "Bring it on, princess."

She bit back all the most awful swear words she knew because—

She. Was. A. Classy. Lady.

Argh! She turned and stalked out the door.

~ ~ ~

Claire was not about to accuse Hailey or anyone else in the book club of snitching to the press. The sooner she found out who was behind it, the sooner she could relax around Jake. And she really wanted to enjoy him. It had been so long since she'd felt really comfortable with a man. So long since she'd felt that spike of desire just from a look or a touch. And he understood the need to keep them out of the spotlight.

She headed back to her trailer for a short break, her silent shadow following her as she thought back to the day Ty had given her the message that Josh knew who she was. Blake and the usual crew had been with her. She had a good relationship with the crew, and Blake had never done anything to hurt her before. Though Blake had been extra bitchy and diva-like on set lately. This was the first time she'd directed him. Did he have a problem with her being the boss? He'd signed on for all of the Fierce trilogy movies. Why would he risk it? Maybe he thought he was untouchable, in no danger of being fired. *Oh, fuck.* She nearly slapped her forehead. It all made sense. Blake had nothing to lose. He could do whatever the hell he wanted because he knew the fans wouldn't accept a substitute Damon. Everyone loved him for the role. She couldn't very well use a different Damon for the second and third movies of the trilogy.

She went inside the trailer, not liking what she knew she had to do. If Blake was leaking stuff to the press, stabbing her in the back, she had to know before it completely torpedoed the movie. She took a deep breath and made the arrangements for a private lunch meeting in her trailer the next day. Frank would be stationed right outside if she needed him. She didn't think Blake was the violent type, but you could never be too careful.

The next day, Blake arrived right on time with a no-carb, high-protein lunch—rare steak and spinach. He smiled. "It's been too long since we had a quiet lunch just the two of us."

The last time had been when she'd talked to him about taking the role of Damon. "Too long," she agreed, taking a seat with her own lunch of salad with salmon and two skinny breadsticks. Her stomach turned, knowing what she had to ask him, and she knew she couldn't eat.

"How you like working here so far?" she asked.

"Great," he said, slicing into his steak. Blood oozed from the rare meat and pooled on the white plate. He shoved the steak in his mouth and pointed the gleaming knife at her, his expression hard. "Anything you need to tell me?"

She licked her dry lips, her gut churning. "No. Production schedule is on track."

She'd wait until he was finished with the knife, clear the table, and then broach the true purpose of their visit. She knew she had a vivid imagination—knife, blood, murder—but her gut never steered her wrong.

She quickly moved the conversation to his favorite topic—himself. He happily talked about his career and major interviews he'd scored, all while wolfing down his steak. He picked at the spinach and shoved the plate back.

"I'll have this taken care of," she said, gathering the plate, knife, and fork, and stepping outside to hand it off to Frank. She leaned her head out and whispered, "Tuck this somewhere."

Frank didn't question it. Merely took the dishes that were not in his job description and returned to being vigilant.

She stepped back inside but remained by the door. "Blake, these stories about me sneaking around with a bartender are doing serious damage to our movie buzz."

"I know. That's why I suggested we go out to that premiere. Turn it back around."

"Look, I'm just going to come out and say this. Only a few people know I went out with him. And you were one of them."

Blake's expression remained impassive. "So? Crew was there too."

"I already questioned them. They all swore they'd never said a word."

"I don't like what you're accusing me of. I'm a professional."

"I'm going to ask you this once and I want you to be honest. Did you tell the press that I went out in disguise with Josh Campbell?"

"Claire, be serious. Why would I—"

"Just answer the question!"

He stood, palms up, a conciliatory gesture at odds with the barely banked hatred simmering in his sharp blue eyes. "You're psycho."

"You don't like answering to a woman boss. You wanted your own production company, but you can't get it off the ground—"

"I've got stuff in the works."

"No, you don't. I know *everything*," she bluffed. "I know it was you who leaked the Josh thing." She didn't know, but the hair on the back of her neck was standing straight up and deep in her gut she knew.

He crossed his arms. "You can't fire me. I have a contract for the trilogy."

"I can buy out your contract and replace you." In theory, that was true. In practice, tough to come up with the funds. Blake wasn't cheap.

"No," Blake said, suddenly appeasing. "We'll make more appearances together. The fans of the franchise will go nuts. They'll forget all about your disguise thing."

"You want more appearances together to raise your own profile. That's what all this was about. To get investors in your production company. Don't you see how you're shooting yourself in the foot? You think you're just bringing me down a notch? You're screwing up all the good PR buzz we had for this movie. That doesn't come cheap."

He gave her a slick smile that made her sick. "Let me make it up to you."

"How? You're killing my movie—"

"Your movie?" He jabbed a finger at her. "That's the problem right there. Your movie, your production company. All high and mighty, bossing everyone around—"

"Get out." She opened the door and gestured for him to go.

"Bitch! You'll be sorry."

He stormed out.

"I already am," she said to herself. She went to the window and watched Frank escorting Blake a distance away. Blake shook him off and headed to his own trailer.

Now what? They were a month away from wrapping production and she didn't have the budget to reshoot with someone else. She was stuck with him. She paced the length of the trailer. She couldn't imagine working with him for two more years, knowing he secretly hated her. Who knew what else he might do to sabotage her?

She wanted to tell Jake. To make sure he knew she'd found the culprit and to apologize for accusing him. She had his number now that he'd texted her. She texted and stared at her phone, willing him to respond. She shook her head, such a normal thing to do, texting a guy and waiting for a response. He was probably working. She sighed and set the phone down. She should eat.

She'd just finished lunch when her cell rang. She snagged it, already feeling better seeing Jake's name on the screen.

"Hey," she said. "It was Blake who told the press about Jenny and Josh. I'm sorry I accused you."

"Ah, fine, you're forgiven," Jake said. "Paranoid movie star."

She laughed. "Thank you, bigheaded CEO."

He chuckled. "So did you fire Blake?"

She sighed. "I'm stuck with him. I can't afford to buy him out of his contract. He's locked in for all three movies."

He whistled a long, sympathetic tone. "That sucks."

"That's show biz."

A silence fell.

"Well," they said at the same time.

She laughed. "I'll see you tomorrow for dinner if you're free. The premiere with Blake is off."

"Sounds good."

"Okay. I'll arrange everything and text you the details. Ciao."

"Come on. Ciao? Could you be more pretentious?"

"Could you be more judgmental?"

He groaned long and loud. "How long until we can get out all this pent-up aggravation and channel it properly?"

"You're a beast."

"I am."

She smiled and held the phone closer. "I kinda like beasts."

"I know you do. I had your number from day one."

"You did not."

"All right, not day one Jenny. Day one Claire."

"I looked you up. You didn't tell me you were named Sexiest Bachelor in Silicon Valley."

"I thought that went without saying."

She laughed. "I can't believe I just had a horrible betrayal from the guy I'm stuck with for the next two years and then you call and I can't stop smiling."

"Get used to it. Ciao, baby."

She grinned. "Ciao."

She hung up and left her trailer, nearly giddy with something that felt very close to love. She'd been in love a time or two, once in high school, too young too soon, and once while she was a struggling actress with another actor. That last one ended when she got her big break and her boyfriend didn't. This felt different. Bigger. All capital letters kind of LOVE. She was getting goofy.

Her assistant rushed up to her as soon as she got back to the set. "Blake's gone. We can't find him anywhere. I think he left the estate."

Dammit. He had a contract, and they needed him today.

She shook her head, coming down from the clouds. "Get his agent on the phone."

~ ~ ~

Jake felt like a double agent with the hoops he had to go through just to have dinner with Claire. No wonder she was paranoid. He had to meet her at the back entrance of her hotel and take a Mercedes with tinted windows through some back-alley route to the service entrance of the restaurant where her assistant had made a reservation under a false name. Her bodyguard came along for the ride, barely saying two words to Jake. Once at the restaurant, they were quickly escorted through the kitchen, where the workers didn't even blink at their presence, and then down a flight of stairs to a basement room with three small tables and three waiters. The space was cozy with dark wood paneling and glowing wall sconces.

He recognized one couple at the other two tables—a big-name actress with her rock-star boyfriend; the other table had two young beautiful people who could have been actors, musicians, or models. It seemed to be the place to go for the beautiful couples looking for privacy. Claire waved to the actress, her smile bright. He lifted his chin in acknowledgement and settled his hand on Claire's lower back, guiding her to the only empty table. Claire looked stunningly beautiful, as anyone would expect from *the* Claire Jordan, in a sleeveless dress, turquoise on top, gold on the skirt. Her sexy gold heels had skinny straps that wrapped around her ankles.

Not that he didn't appreciate her efforts, but he'd been just as drawn to her as Jenny with no designer anything and no makeup at all. He figured she had enough people in her life gushing over her beauty so when he first saw her all glammed up, he'd merely said, "Nice dress." To which she'd said, "Nice shirt." It was a white button-down tailor-made to his measurements. And that was enough with the compliments.

Once they were settled at the table, he leaned across it and spoke in a low tone meant for Claire's ears alone. "No wonder you have such a big head. It's like you're the president or something."

She puckered her lips to the side, looking adorably put out. "Ya know, insulting your date isn't the way to beast mode."

He chuckled. "Beast mode after this. Guarantee

it."

"And you say I'm the one with the big head. Haven't you heard of taking things slow?"

"I'm not good at waiting. Neither are you. Otherwise we wouldn't have—" he raised his voice to a falsetto "—*hoo-hoo* on our first date, Jenny."

She laughed, the throaty, husky sound he loved. "Keep your voice down."

He glanced at the menu. "You always eat dinner at nine o'clock?"

"It was the only time I could get. Griffin Huntley reserved the entire room for him and his wife before this. It was their date night." That was a huge rock star. Now he was impressed.

Jake looked around the cozy space. "Griffin Huntley eats here? It must be good."

"Yes, it is, sir," the waiter, a tall, thin man said, appearing suddenly at their table.

Jake smoothly covered. "The lady and I will have your best champagne. We're celebrating."

"Very good, sir." The waiter left.

Claire tilted her head with a sunny smile. "And what are we celebrating?"

A rush of affection surged through him. She was everything—sweet and fiery, sexy in an effortless way. Glamorous, yes, but not superficial. There were layers. He was a goner, even with the Jenny/Claire twist.

He took her hand and stroked the underside of her wrist. "The beginning of something great. At least I think it will be great. I fell for Jenny, but the jury's still out on you."

Her hazel eyes danced with amusement. "I could run circles around Jenny."

He brushed his lips across her knuckles and felt someone staring. He looked over to where her bodyguard, Frank, was standing at the entrance to the room like a soldier. Their eyes met, and Frank's gaze flicked away.

Jake leaned across the table and whispered, "So does Frank just stand there the whole meal?"

"Yes," she whispered back. "He always stays by the main access point to a room with a visual on any alternate access points."

"And does he go with you to your…" He hesitated, but he had to know. "How do you have sex?"

She grinned devilishly. "The usual way."

He didn't laugh. Frank was creeping him out the way he stared. He kept his voice low. "So he's like right outside the door?"

She shook her head and whispered, "He'll check to make sure the room is okay, and then he stays in his room below mine."

"Can he hear everything?"

"I hope not. I don't know."

He thought about that, glancing over at the stone-faced giant again. Talk about a cock block. "So he's always with you?"

She nodded and whispered, "It's necessary for my safety. And his number is programmed in my cell. I'm supposed to wear this emergency one-touch bracelet to contact him too, but it's ugly." She wrinkled her nose.

He bit back a laugh. The woman had a shadow that she fully accepted but not to the point of messing with her outfit. "Oh, it's ugly."

"Yeah."

"So you only like fashionable security devices?"

She took a sip of water, hiding a smile. "And there's so few of those."

A basket of warm bread arrived. He offered her the basket, and she shook her head. "Too many carbs."

He took a slice of sourdough for himself and slathered it with butter. "Jenny wouldn't care about carbs."

"Jenny's not doing a sex scene on film in her teeny groin cover."

He closed his eyes. He did not want to think about Claire nearly nude with another man even if it was simulated sex. He opened his eyes to find her staring.

"Does it bother you?" she asked.

"Nah. I'm sure he sucks in the sack."

"It's not sexy at all. It's very technical, getting the staging right. Plus the crew is right there."

He changed the subject. "So what's next for you? Where do you go after you finish filming this movie?"

"We wrap on *Fierce Longing* two days before Thanksgiving. That's ironclad. Everyone has plans to fly home for the holiday. I'll do some postproduction in LA, then Vancouver for three months for another film. I'll be in Connecticut again next October to film the second movie of the trilogy. We're staggering the Fierce movies one a year. There's *Fierce Longing*, *Fierce Craving*, and *Fierce Loving*."

He took a bite of bread and chewed. "I should read those books. They sound dirty."

Her eyes lit up. "They are. But also a really powerful story of love and redemption."

The waiter arrived with their champagne, opening it with a muted *pop* and then pouring a small amount in each of their glasses.

Claire took a sip. "Wonderful, thank you."

The waiter smiled. "Very good." He poured a little more in each of their glasses and left.

Claire raised her glass. "To love and redemption."

"I'm not sure what that means in this context, but…" He went to clink glasses, but she held hers back.

"It means we're both redeeming ourselves by

showing our true selves."

His voice came out husky with the emotion clogging his throat. "And the love?"

She gave him a small smile. "I don't know. I had some feelings for Josh, but the jury's still out on you."

He couldn't help but smile. "Touché."

She smirked. He clinked his glass against hers and they drank.

He set his glass down. "Where do you live when you're not filming?"

She lifted one shoulder. "I have a place in Aspen, one in San Francisco—"

"I live in San Francisco. Well, close by. Do the neighborly thing and stop by."

"I'll bring a picnic."

He gazed at her warmly, remembering their first picnic. "Just bring you."

She shook her head. "Why do I feel like you're too good to be true? Like any moment this is all going to go poof!" She flexed her fingers in the air.

"Like you're on a prank show."

She looked around suspiciously.

"You're not. This is real." He took both her hands in his. "As real as it gets."

The waiter returned with a first course of salad.

After he left, Jake watched Claire take tiny bites of salad and chew slowly. She didn't have an ounce of fat on her. He wouldn't mind seeing her with soft curves. He understood, though. If he was filming in the buff, he'd be working out round the clock and watching that scale.

She looked up. "I told Hailey about you and Josh switching places."

"Yeah? What'd she say? Did she still like dinner? It was a three-star Michelin-rated restaurant."

"Oh, that's what he did? I didn't know how he taught her a lesson. Huh. So he just took her to dinner, pretending to be you? She's so mad I thought it was much worse. All she'll say is he'll never date in this town again."

He burst out laughing. He could just imagine Hailey plotting some revenge. Probably tell everyone Josh had an STD or something.

"You don't mess with Hailey," Claire said.

Jake shook his head. "He took her out to show her she really wanted him not the billionaire brother."

"You're a billionaire?"

"You didn't look up my portfolio?"

"No. I just looked up the basics—marital status, criminal record, sexiest bachelor titles."

He chuckled. "I fell out of the ten-figure club recently. Anyway, back to Josh. Get this. He went through all that elaborate setup, but then he never did the big reveal, never rubbed it in her face. He just took her to dinner, took her home, and that's it."

"There must've been more to it than that." She ate some more salad, looking thoughtful. "She's furious. Something must've happened."

"If it did, he's not telling."

"I'll work on her. Women talk about stuff, especially Hailey. It's really not like her not to share all the details. She is all about details." She pursed her lips. "And he sounds like a jerk."

"Hey, that's my twin."

"I know, but—"

"Yeah, it was a jerky thing to do. He's all twisted up over Hailey. It's really simple. You like a woman, you ask her out, seduce her, and screw her brains out. That's my philosophy."

She bit back a smile, but he could see the laughter dancing in her eyes. "You might've missed a step there."

He pretended to consider this. "No, I don't think so. That's about it."

She laughed. "I shouldn't encourage you."

"You really should."

Their salad plates were whisked away the moment they finished. The entrees arrived a few minutes later. Everything was farm-to-table and organic. Claire had salmon with roasted vegetables. Again, no carbs. He had steak with sweet potato puree. He remembered the look of ecstasy on her face when he'd hand-fed her chocolate cake on their picnic. Now that he thought about it, she only had three bites. And that cake was fantastic.

"Don't you miss carbs?" he asked.

"I have them between films. It's fine."

He sliced into the steak, perfectly medium well. "So what happened with that guy's agent?" He knew he wasn't supposed to say names when they were out in public, but he was curious what happened with Blake.

"Later," she said.

He nodded once. "Got it."

They finished dinner, conversation easy between them just like when they were Jenny and Josh. It only made him more certain that this thing between them was real, always had been, and it would build from there. He coaxed Claire into having a drink at his friend's bar downtown. He'd reserved the private room on the third floor, a favorite place of his to take clients or friends. Occasionally a woman.

On the drive over, she snuggled against his side and filled him in on Blake.

"I told his agent he was in breach of contract, threatened with my lawyer, and Blake shows up two hours later drunk off his ass."

He squeezed her shoulder. "That's terrible."

"Yup. And then today he showed up an hour late, hungover and snarling at everyone. He fired his assistant and then threw a fit that no one brought him his specialty coffee, which was what his assistant would have done if he hadn't been fired." She let out a long sigh. "He's been harassing me about Josh too, saying the guy just wants me for publicity for his bar."

"You didn't tell him about me?"

"I don't want anyone to know about you. They have enough to talk about with the Josh thing."

"We should go public. It's not fair to Josh. He's been dodging the press and it stresses him out to have a crowd near him."

"But he works at a bar. Isn't he always in a crowd of people? Or at weddings?"

"He can handle the bar because there's a barrier between him and other people, but it's different when he steps outside and there's a bunch of reporters. I imagine he sticks to the edges of the room at weddings."

She sank further into the seat. "I don't want people to know about us. It'll ruin it. I just found you, and I want to keep us private. It's especially important for the fans to keep the focus on Damon and Mia." He didn't like the way she let the press dictate her life, especially when his brother had to deal with the fallout.

He shifted to meet her eyes. "Forever?"

"No, not forever. For a while. Until I'm sure that we're at a level that it doesn't matter what the press says. And that everything is all set for the movie." She sighed. "It's better this way. You don't understand what you're in for." Her voice dropped, sad and resigned. "It's a nightmare."

He tried to lighten the mood. "You don't even know what you're in for with all my Silicon Valley peeps. Talk about a nightmare."

The corners of her mouth tilted up. "Oh yeah?"

"Oh yeah." He played with a lock of her hair. "Computer bugs that'll keep you up at night. Shareholder meetings that'll put you to sleep."

She wrapped an arm around his middle. "Tell me what you do. I read it's something to do with sharing information."

"Your Google fu powers are impressive."

She laughed. He told her, explaining why he'd started the company and the technology's uses all over the world. He also told her about the offers he'd had to buy his company, so she'd know that he could be flexible with where he lived and how he spent his time for a future with her. Though he didn't state the future-with-her part out loud. He never laid all his cards on the table this early in the game.

"Impressive," she said.

He dipped his head to whisper in her ear, "Now if you'll just say that tonight when I drop my pants."

She smacked his shoulder and laughed.

They were off to a flying start. A second start, actually, even better than the first because it was real.

CHAPTER THIRTEEN

Claire was a little nervous about the unexpected stop for a drink with Jake—she normally gave a heads-up ahead of her arrival and Frank scouted out the location. But, at the same time, she wanted to continue their date. She hated feeling like she had to stop having fun just because she was famous. It turned out that the bar was the Irish pub they'd stopped at on their second Jenny and Josh date. Jake described how to get to the private room on the third floor to both her and Frank, who was sitting up front with the driver.

"So I take it you know the owner?" she asked.

He laced his fingers with hers in that easy affectionate way he had. "My friend Marcus owns it. I was one of his original investors. He paid me back within the year, but I always get the VIP treatment."

Okay, it would be okay. It was a controlled environment. He knew the owner. The room was reserved just for them, and she knew Frank would stick close.

"Relax," Jake said. "You're not going to a firing squad. We're just going to have a drink, have a good time."

She didn't reply. He had no idea the kind of crazy shit she had to deal with from rabid fans wanting a piece of her. If he stuck around long enough, he'd see. It wasn't just pictures or autographs. It was hands grabbing, wanting her hair or a piece of her clothing. The men who had erotic fantasies about her and had to touch. That was why she had Frank. At times she wanted a whole bunch of Franks so she could move unaccosted in a bubble of protection.

The car pulled up to the building. Frank got out alone to check things out ahead of time while the driver circled the block.

Jake kept trying to distract her, kissing her neck, but she couldn't relax enough to enjoy it.

She shoved his shoulder. "Not now."

He slid a hand into her hair, his eyes hot on hers, and waited for one breathless moment. She blinked, mesmerized. And then his mouth claimed hers, aggressive and rough enough that she could think of nothing but the heat and taste of him. A rare delicious butterfly feeling in her stomach reminded her that Jake was special.

He pulled away when the car stopped moving and gave her a slow sexy smile. "We're here."

Frank opened the back door of the car and poked his head in. "There's some paps. We're gonna move fast. Ready?"

Shit. How did the paparazzi know she was here? They were already crowding in close to the car.

She turned to Jake. "We have to hustle. Frank will get us in safe."

"I'm not running."

"Just move quickly, okay?"

He frowned. "Why? Because of some asshole with a camera?"

"Just do it," she hissed and exited the car. Flashes went off, nearly blinding her in the dark of night. She turned to find Jake standing, straightening his shirt, and striding at his usual pace, his expression hard. Almost like he was daring them to get too close.

And then Frank had her by the elbow, keeping her partially hidden, and she rushed into the building, straight through to an employees-only door, through a storage area, and then upstairs and through a door marked Private. Jake wasn't with them. What was he doing? Was he talking to the paps? Giving them a story? Dammit.

She arrived on the third floor with a fully stocked bar, where a bartender, a large man with short-cropped dark hair around her age, stood at the ready. It was the man who'd greeted Jake so warmly the last time they were here. He smiled at her. She gave him a tight smile back. There were a half dozen round tables and a pool table. Still no Jake.

Finally he arrived, strolling on in. Frank stepped out to wait just outside the door.

"What took you so long?" she demanded.

Jake headed over to the bar. "What do you want to drink?"

She tapped her foot. She couldn't scream at him in front of the bartender, who was even now greeting Jake like a long-lost brother.

Jake looked over at her. "Come meet Marcus. He's serving us this evening."

Marcus grabbed Jake's shoulder and gave it a shake.

She slapped on her gracious meet-the-fans face and crossed over to them. "Hello, nice to meet you, Marcus. I'm—"

"Claire Jordan. I know." Marcus grinned. "What're you doing with this guy?"

She raised her brows. "I'm beginning to wonder that myself."

Jake faked a jab to the heart. "Ooh!" He went behind the bar with Marcus. "She's mad because I wouldn't run in here like she wanted. I don't take orders."

"It wasn't an order," she said between her teeth. "It was for your safety."

Jake shook his head and looked around behind the bar. "You can't let some guy with a camera dictate the way you live your life. They're going to talk about you anyway. Do what you want."

"It's not that easy," she said.

"Yeah, it is."

Marcus pulled a beer bottle out and handed it to him. Jake popped the top and took a swig. She would've ground her teeth if they weren't so expensive to repair.

"Did you talk to them?" she asked Jake tightly. The hell with her gracious fan face.

"I'm sensing some tension," Marcus said. "Here you go." He lined up a chilled bottle of white and a bottle of red on top of the bar. "Jake will pour. They're both excellent. Nice to meet you, Claire."

"You too," she said. "Thank you."

Marcus headed out, chuckling to himself.

The moment he left the room, she let Jake have it. "What did you do in the ten minutes it took you to get up here?"

"Relax. It was nothing. I was just trying to show you that you can act like a normal human being and nothing bad will happen." He gestured to the wine bottles. "What do you want, white or red?"

"What did you do?" she pressed.

"Nothing. Geez, you're paranoid. Can we get back to the part where we're having a date? I didn't tell those people to show up. This is a happening section of town. They probably hang around all the time."

She crossed her arms, still pissed that he didn't follow directions. She had a lot more experience with this than he did. He walked around the bar, pulled her arms apart and wrapped his arms around her.

His voice rumbled in her ear. "Come on, have a drink with me."

She blew out an aggravated breath, but she didn't pull away. It was rare for her to be held, and she felt too good to move. He started humming some unknown tune before taking her hand in his while his other hand slid to her lower back. Her anger seeped away as he led her in a waltz.

She sighed and rested her cheek against his warm chest, breathing in his woodsy spice scent. Maybe she'd overreacted. He wasn't used to the way things were done.

"That's more like it," he said, the sound reverberating in his chest.

For some reason, his cockiness amused her more than irritated her. Maybe because she admired his confidence. Some men were intimidated by her big name and were more aggressive to make up for it, a move she always saw for what it was—all bluster, no substance. Jake had an abundance of confidence but with real success to back it up. She was starting to believe that meeting him instead of his twin had been a twist of fate with a strong dose of destiny. He didn't need to know that, though. Much too early to expose her heart.

She lifted her head, a little alarmed at the intensity of all she felt for him. "Okay, I'll take that drink."

He pulled her hand over her head and twirled her around. "Since Marcus split, the big weenie, I guess I'll be your bartender this evening." He stopped twirling her when she faced him again, gave her a tender kiss, then nipped her lower lip, giving her a jolt. He kept surprising her, sweet with an edge that kept her on her toes.

He strode over to the bar and lifted the bottle of red. "I'm sensing you're in a red mood, the color of passion."

"Did anyone ever tell you how very subtle you are?"

He grinned and unscrewed the cork. "Surprisingly, no. You're the first."

She shook her head with a smile.

"Pick a table where you'd like to be debauched," he said. "I'll be right over."

She looked over at the dark wood tables and around the room, considering the crazy idea for a moment. There were only two windows covered by long dark red drapes. And, of course, Frank standing on the other side of the door.

She took a seat on one of the round bar stools. "Keep dreaming."

He handed her a glass of wine. She took a sip. "This is really good."

"I wouldn't take you some place with bad wine. Marcus knows the good stuff."

"You invest in a lot of bars?"

"No. Just this one. He's one of the blood brothers I told you about."

Ah. She wondered if she'd ever meet his family. Maybe if they all went someplace private. Like her hideaway in Maine. Her family was scattered. Her brother in London. Her parents retired in North Carolina.

"What're you thinking about?" he asked, taking the bar stool next to her.

"I'm wondering where we go from here."

"Easy. We're going back to your hotel."

"Oh, really?" So arrogantly confident. So right.

He took a pull on his beer. "We both know where this is going."

She huffed and rolled her eyes in a big display of

yeah, right.

He tugged on a lock of her hair. "You forget I grew up with Mad. I know all about the big show." He leaned close. "The drama. Don't bother to hide how much you want me. It's in big neon letters over your head—do me."

She couldn't help but laugh.

He took another long swallow of beer, his eyes hot on hers. "Fuck the drink. Let's go."

"Now, wait a minute, you made a big deal about continuing our date and that's what we're going to do. I didn't just face the gauntlet of paps and stress of an unplanned outing to rush out of here."

"Okay."

She nearly fell off the barstool in shock at his easy capitulation. "Okay."

She reached for her wineglass when he snagged it first. He raised it to her lips, giving her a sip, watching her with a heated intensity that made her gulp the wine down. The merlot was rich with a hint of cherries, warming her. He set the glass back on the bar, and then he traced her lips with one finger, and then traced them again with his tongue. Her lips parted on a sigh, her body heavy and liquid with desire. His tongue swept inside, thrusting in imitation of where she knew this was heading. She moaned and wrapped her arms around his neck. She hadn't gotten nearly enough when he lifted his head.

"I like this drink we're having," he said, his voice gravelly. "Let's have some more."

She nodded.

This time, he pushed her legs apart, making her dress ride further up her thighs, and stood between them before lifting the glass to her lips. He gazed at her mouth and set the glass on the bar with an audible clunk before they slammed together, their mouths hungry. Desire spiked within her as his hand slid up her inner thigh, grazing the edge of her silk thong, making her crazed.

"Okay, let's go," she said.

He gave her a rather smug look. "But we didn't finish your drink, and it tastes so good." He was dragging this out, playing with her like a lusty cat with a lusty mouse.

She grabbed his ass and pulled him close. "I changed my mind. Consent, desire, intent, all a go."

He laughed, a low, wicked sound, as he pulled away just enough for her to make a mewl of protest. "That's Josh." His fingers unexpectedly slid under her thong and one long stroke made her shudder. "Who're you with?" he prompted.

"Jake," she gasped as his finger stroked unerringly to pleasure central. He made lazy circles, drawing further away from where she wanted him.

"Jake just wants proof that you're ready and willing." He held up one wet finger and sucked. Her breath shuddered out. Then he dragged that same finger over her bottom lip, past her teeth, and into her mouth. She tasted herself, and she liked it. She sucked his finger, watching his eyes dilate with desire.

He dropped his finger and kissed her again, his hands everywhere, his mouth hard and demanding. She wanted him in that desperate way she had the first time she was with him. She'd never wanted anyone like this before.

She tore her mouth away. "Jake. Yes. Ready, willing. Now."

One corner of his mouth lifted. "But we didn't finish your excellent wine."

She grabbed the glass and drained it. He chuckled that low, knowing laugh of his that said he knew he had her. She didn't care. She slowly licked her lips, tempting, driving him. He stopped smiling and grabbed her suddenly, pulling her off the bar stool. He pushed her dress up to her waist and lifted her, kissing her passionately. She wrapped her legs tightly around him, loving the friction of his hardness against her. He broke the kiss and walked with her toward the door.

"Wait," she said, coming back to her reality. "Frank's right there. The paps. You have to put me down."

He palmed her bottom, the touch searing her bare skin. "They don't want a shot of this fine ass?"

"That's exactly what they want. Put me down."

"But you feel so good. I wish I could do you here." Still carrying her, still palming her ass. The movement of him walking made her rub against him so deliciously that for one crazy moment she wished he could do her here too.

"Good things come to those who wait," she said.

He set her down. "You're the good thing who's going to come."

"I like the way you think." She grabbed his hand and dashed out into the hallway. Frank didn't seem at all surprised by their sudden appearance, and her cheeks heated, wondering how much he'd heard.

"We're heading back to the hotel," Claire told Frank.

The three of them headed downstairs and then Frank hustled her to the car. She kept a firm grip on Jake's hand, even as a couple of photographers leaned close to get the shot.

She and Jake were both quiet on the drive to the hotel. She was bursting with anticipation, turned on and not able to do anything about it for at least twenty minutes. She didn't know why Jake was quiet. But his hand was firmly on her upper thigh. And his occasional looks over at her were full of promised seduction.

The moment they were alone in her suite, she launched herself at him. He caught her and kissed her with an intensity that made her breathless and dizzy.

"Which way to the bedroom?" he asked.

"Right, then left."

"Got it."

He found the master bedroom, brought her in, and shut the door behind them. "Put some music on."

She kissed his neck, tasting him, sucking and biting. He was like the most delicious dessert. But this kind she could have as much as she wanted.

"Because of that cock block downstairs," he said, tugging on her hair. "I need some noise besides you screaming in ecstasy."

She stilled. "Screaming?" A shiver went through her at the dark promise in his eyes.

"You didn't think I was going to go easy on you this second time, did you? That was Josh and Jenny. Gloves are off, baby."

Her pulse raced, feverish heat making her breath ragged. He muttered a curse before pinning her up against the door and kissing her breathless, grinding against her. He kissed his way up her neck and spoke against her lips. "You look at me like that, I can barely think." He yanked up her dress and pulled it over her head. His gaze raked her from head to toe as she stood there in bra, thong, and heels. "I didn't get to see you before. Fuck." He moved fast, flicking the clasp of the bra open with one expert move, peeling it off her, and then sliding the thong down and off. "Leave the heels."

She stood, waiting, desperate for his touch as his gaze took her in again from head to toe and then lingered on her sex.

"Touch me," she said.

He didn't hesitate, his mouth slamming over hers, his hands on her waist, sliding over the curve of her hips. She wrapped her arms around his neck, glad to have his heat back, pressing fully against her. His hand thrust between her legs, cupping her. She moaned softly and sank back against the door. And then he broke the kiss, watching her as he stroked and thrust with his fingers. She rocked, moving to his rhythm, letting herself feel all the pleasure he gave. Her moans got louder as his fingers became more demanding. She tensed as everything coiled within her, tight and hot. His mouth covered hers suddenly, swallowing her moans as he pushed her further and further to the edge. And then she flew, rocking against his hand, her cries muffled by his mouth.

He cupped her still-tingling sex and lifted his head. "I can't believe you came so fast. That was too easy. You gotta go deeper than that."

"Deeper?" she whispered. It was rare for her to even have an orgasm. She had with him before, but too many times she'd felt used and abandoned after sex.

He still cupped her as his other hand stroked down her throat. "Like your whole world dims and then explodes. And you're shattered into quivering pieces." He dipped his head and gave her earlobe a tug between his teeth. "And then I'll put you back together and break you open again until your breath is ragged and your legs are wobbly and all you can say is my name."

"Jesus," she whispered.

He gave her a wicked smile. "It's Jake." And then he kissed her again, his tongue sweeping inside in delicious possession. Her knees went weak, her body humming with desire as the kiss went on and on, his warm hands roaming all over her.

He broke the kiss. "Put some music on. You're going to be screaming this time."

She couldn't even speak, just stared at him.

He backed away and put his palms in the air. "I'm going to the bed. You're going to put the music on."

He started unbuttoning his shirt, so she stayed for the show. He stopped and looked around. "You don't have a radio alarm clock. Where can we get some music? Put the TV on. Something. I can't work under these conditions!"

That made her laugh. "Okay, I got it. I have a speaker dock." She grabbed her cell, quickly fetched the speaker dock from the other room, and plugged it in on the nightstand. "What do you like to listen to?"

"Something loud," he said from across the room.

She had workout music, dance music, and soothing music. She chose dance music because it had a nice hard beat. He came up behind her, tossed a condom on the nightstand, and wrapped his arms around her.

"Perfect," he said before kissing the side of her neck. His hands roamed over her body, stroking her breasts and down to her stomach, across to her hips. She arched back into him, an invitation for more. His heat left her back.

She turned to find him pulling back the covers and getting into bed, lying on his back. Yes! She ripped open the condom and rolled it on him.

"I'm not going to ask how you're so good at that," he said.

She straddled him, raised herself up, but he stopped her, hands on her hips. "Not yet," he said.

She tried to move, but he had her in a firm grip. "Why not?"

"Because you didn't go deep enough." He moved her up his body as he slid down.

"Jake," she protested. This was so dirty. She didn't

want to—

"Ride my mouth," he said before his mouth closed over her center. She cried out as he sucked hard, and she reached out to hang onto the headboard. His hands were on her hips, moving her over him, working her with his wicked mouth. She trembled, gripping the headboard hard, trying to hold herself up, but he wouldn't let her, holding her open and exposed and close. A white-hot surge of pleasure rocked her, making the room dim, the beat of the music moving her hips now as she surrendered to her body's craving for more and more and more. She screamed as the climax snuck up on her, explosive in its intensity, rocking her to her core. He kept going, bringing shockwaves of pleasure until she was spent.

He slid out from under her and went behind her, tugging her hips back against him. "So good," he murmured.

She rested her cheek on the cool pillow, sweaty tendrils of hair falling in her face. He entered her slowly, filling her, pushing deep until she'd taken him to the hilt. She moaned softly.

He covered her and pushed her hair from her face. Then he kissed her shoulder. "You can give me more."

"I've never come twice before," she admitted. Most men didn't make the effort that Jake did. "I'm not sure I can give you more."

"You can," he said with cocky confidence and rocked into her, bringing another wave of pleasure.

"Jake…"

He rocked into her again, taking his time, easy strokes that brought gentle waves of pleasure to her body. "I love that you can only say my name."

"I can—"

He thrust deep, yanking her hips back onto him.

"Jake!" she cried out.

And then he was rocking her, stroking her on the inside, making her feverish, shaking with need. He kept her there, playing with her, until she was begging for her release. He grunted and thrust hard, over and over, pushing her to the peak that seemed just out of reach. Her world narrowed down to the rush of sensation centered deep inside, the thudding of her heart, her ragged breath, the heat at her back. And then her world went dark as a surge of pleasure ripped through her, leaving her panting and shaking under him. He thrust deep and held her hips tight against him as he climaxed with a long, low groan.

Her mind was a haze of bliss. She could think of nothing but the man who brought her such incredible pleasure. "Jake," she whispered.

He pulled out and rolled to his back. She collapsed on the mattress. He threw an arm over her back. Long moments passed while they caught their breath. He hit the power button on the speaker dock and the room went quiet.

She turned off the light, pulled the covers up, and snuggled against his side. "That was even better than the first time," she said, still reeling from all he'd made her feel.

He didn't respond. She lifted her head to look at him. It was hard to make him out in the dark. Then she heard a soft snore.

She settled her head against his chest. "I'm falling for you," she whispered in the dark. It felt good to express what she felt and even better knowing it couldn't be used against her.

CHAPTER FOURTEEN

The next morning Claire woke from the sexiest dream, near orgasm. Her eyes flew open as she realized it was real. Jake was spooning her, stroking between her legs in gentle circles.

"Jake," she whispered, and he increased the pressure, sending her over with a sharp cry.

He rolled her to her back and smiled down at her. "Wake-up call."

She reached for him, the smile on her face so big it hurt her cheeks. "C'mere and have your way with me."

"That was always the plan," he said, rolling on top of her and thrusting inside.

She held onto him tightly, their joining fast and furious and close. She'd never felt so close to another person.

He lifted his head, his dark eyes gazing into hers. "God, Claire."

"I know."

He entwined his fingers with hers and pulled her arms up over her head, his gaze never leaving hers as he made love to her. That was what this felt like, so much more than sex, a soul-deep joining. She lifted her hips, taking him deeper. He groaned and pumped hard and fast, sending them both hurtling into oblivion.

He collapsed on the bed next to her. She peeked over at him, wide awake and happy. "You're not falling asleep again, are you?"

"Sex makes me sleepy," he murmured. His eyes closed, a small smile on his gorgeous face.

She pulled the cover over him and headed to the bathroom to shower and get ready. By the time she got back to the bedroom, he was awake and checking his cell phone.

She sat next to him on the bed. "Anything interesting?"

He looked at her, serious. "Don't freak out, okay?"

A chill went through her. "Why do I not need to freak out?"

He showed her his cell phone screen. There was a picture of the two of them with the headline: Twins for the lucky lady! Claire Jordan out with the bartender's twin, Jake.

Her hand went to her throat. "How did they know?"

He rubbed his forehead. "This is the part where

you don't freak out. I told them last night."

"You told them? Why would you do that?"

"Because they kept asking me about Garner's and I didn't want Josh to have to deal with it anymore. I told you it's stressful for him. So I explained there was a mix-up and it was actually me, his identical twin Jake, who went out with you. It's the truth anyway."

"I can't believe you! I told you I wanted to keep us private!"

"It's not that bad."

"It is bad! Now they're going to make up all kinds of stories about how I'm doing twins. Ménage a twin or whatever you call it."

His lips twitched. "Ménage a trois."

She stood, furious. "This might be funny to you, but it's not to me. You probably did this on purpose to get your name in the headlines. Since you've got those offers on your company. This will just up your status." She should've known. Men always used her like this to make themselves into something bigger.

"Claire, it's not like that. You make it sound like I'm using you for your name."

She crossed her arms. "Aren't you?"

"No." He stood and wrapped his arms around her. "I'm using you for your body."

She jerked away.

"Come on," he said. "I was joking. You're acting

like a prima donna. Not everything's about you."

"This is, Jake! This is very much about me." She grabbed her cell and punched in the code. Ten voice mails, at least a hundred emails with alerts on her name, and seven increasingly frantic texts from her publicist. "I put everything I had into the Fierce trilogy. There's nothing left for a marketing campaign. All I have is the good buzz around me and Blake to make an impact."

"So you can't have a relationship because of a movie? Is that what you're saying?"

She quickly texted her publicist that she was on it. "It's not that simple. This is my career, my business, my future all wrapped up in one." She met his eyes. "Now I have to deal with the fallout while you just walk away carefree. Your net worth just went back to ten figures."

"Why's everything about money with you?" he barked.

"Because that's what people want from me! They want to use me in whatever way it most benefits them."

"Maybe that's what you wanted from me," he said. "That's my experience with women."

"You pig! How dare you accuse me of being a gold digger! I have my own money and you know it."

"No, you don't. You just said it was all invested in

that movie."

"I'll get it back if I can just have a good opening weekend, which means I need good press." Her cell vibrated with a text. She looked at him. "Frank wants to know if I'm okay."

"So tell him you are." His lip curled. "It's like you have a giant babysitter."

She glared at him.

"What? Are you going to pretend I'm doing something to you that'll make him kick me out? I haven't done anything you haven't begged for."

"That's over," she spat. She quickly texted Frank that she was okay. "You should go."

"Just because I don't jump at your command and play your little cloak-and-dagger games to hide from the world doesn't mean I'm against you. I want to be with you."

"On your terms."

"Yes. Because yours are fucked up. You put the press above the people in your life that actually care about you. That's me in case you didn't know!"

She felt like kicking something. She stalked to the pile of his clothes and threw them at him. "You don't understand. If you really cared about me, you would at least *try* to see this from my perspective. I'm a commodity. A brand. And that has to be protected at all costs."

He stared at her for a long moment before he pulled his shirt on. "Maybe your price is too high."

Her knees nearly buckled, and she locked them tight. Because he didn't think she was worth the cost of being with her.

"I want you gone," she said quietly before making a quick exit to the living room where she knew she had to call her publicist. It would be a cascading number of calls after that to settle things down and turn the message.

Claire was on the phone with her screaming publicist for the next several minutes, her blood pressure spiking into the red zone, but she still heard the slam of the front door.

~ ~ ~

Somehow Claire got through the next month of shooting intimate love and fight scenes with Blake. The fight scenes were a helluva lot easier because they hated each other. She was sure Blake was behind all the press reporting that tensions were high on set. He was stabbing them all in the back just so he could vent to someone and get back at her. And she wasn't feeling the least bit loving since Jake ripped her heart out and stomped on it. She hadn't heard from him. He was just gone—poof—too good to be true. Just like she thought.

On the last day of filming, everyone was sentimental for their last time together. She hoped to see some of the crew on the next Fierce movie, but it always depended on the volatile schedules associated with filming.

After cake and a round of champagne toasts, Claire made her way back to her trailer, her silent shadow trailing close by.

"You bitch!" Blake hollered behind her.

She turned. "I'm sorry?"

His face was red. "You put in an offer to buy out my contract? The fans are going to see me as Damon. They won't accept a substitute."

"I don't know what you're talking about."

"Who did you get to replace me?"

"I didn't offer to buy out your contract."

"The hell you didn't. My agent just told me your boyfriend made an offer. Campbell."

She blinked. "Campbell." He didn't. Why would he do that? They weren't even speaking to each other.

"Don't expect me to do any press for this movie. I'm going to say it's a piece of shit."

"No one will want to work with you if you do that."

He rushed at her, but Frank blocked him. "Move along, Blake," Frank said, his tone low and ominous. "Claire, go to your trailer."

On shaky legs, she returned to her trailer. She sank onto a chair, in shock for a full minute. Then she called Jake. "Did you offer to buy out Blake's contract?"

"Nope, not me."

She could hear the smile in his voice. "Yes, you. Don't do that. We need him. And it's a terrible investment anyway."

"How about I chip in for that marketing campaign you're so worried about that you won't even pick up the phone for the best lover you ever had?"

Tears stung her eyes. "You didn't call me either."

"We're a couple of hardheaded tenderhearted souls. A matching pair. And I miss the hell out of you."

Her throat was tight. "I miss you too." She swallowed hard. "But you don't have to invest in my movie to be with me. It's my worry, not yours."

"My investment is in you."

She broke down in tears. She couldn't help it. She'd missed him so much and she never thought he'd make that kind of sacrifice on her behalf. She thought he meant it when he said she wasn't worth it. That the cost to be with her was too high.

"Claire? Are those happy tears?"

She sniffled and grabbed a tissue, wiping her runny nose. Nothing glamorous about Claire Jordan today.

"You said the cost to be with me was too high."

"Yeah, well, the cost is much higher *not* being with you. This month has been hell. I couldn't stop thinking about you because…I love you."

"I love you too!"

"When do you get back to California?"

"Tomorrow."

"Do the neighborly thing and drop by."

She cried a happy sob. "Jake." She swiped at her tears. "I still can't believe you would do all this."

"I told you I wanted to be with you. What, you didn't believe me?"

"No, I didn't."

"I'll sell my company and travel wherever you're filming. We'll make a home together. Two hardheaded, big ego, perfectly matched people."

"Do *not* sell your company because of me."

"What about for our kids?"

She started crying again. "You're just too good to be true."

"You are so right. See you soon."

She hung up, shaking. Then she called Hailey to tell her the good news. Her book club friends would be stopping by the hotel tonight for dinner and to help her pack up her home away from home.

She had her assistant switch the early morning flight the next day from LA to San Francisco. She'd been planning on staying at a hotel in LA for postproduction, but she deserved a small break, and she was desperate to see Jake again.

Claire went a little overboard for her last book club get-together with three kinds of margaritas and sidecar cocktails (in honor of *Fierce Longing*) from the hotel bar, catered food from the best Mexican restaurant in the city, and two flavors of dark chocolate glazed mousse from the best French patisserie. On top of all that, like a total overexcited nerd, Claire arrived in the private lounge early.

She paced the empty lounge. She'd kinda miss the bland gray space. So many happy memories here. The food and drink sat waiting on the bar top, with the dessert chilling in the refrigerator behind the bar. She remembered their first book club meeting. She'd thought they'd sit at the long table on one side of the space, but Hailey had directed them all to grab a chair and sit in a circle instead. Said it was more intimate that way. She was right.

She helped herself to a blood orange margarita, perfect for fall. She should be exhausted. She'd left her room at five a.m. this morning, worked all day, and returned at seven. Instead she was pumped. It reminded her of that excited feeling she got as a kid when she had a slumber party. She put on some celebratory music through her cell phone-speaker dock setup and danced around a bit by herself.

Half an hour later, the front door to the lounge opened. Frank's large shaved head peeked in and he nodded once before stepping back for her friends. They brought life into the dull space, loud and happy.

She rushed forward to hug each and every one of them, suddenly choked up, knowing they'd be saying goodbye.

"Now, none of that," Hailey said. "We're going to keep in touch. You're not getting rid of us that easy."

Julia smiled and squeezed Claire's shoulder. "Besides, Claire has to come back to film *Fierce Craving* and *Fierce Loving*."

"And she and Jake are officially a couple," Hailey said, beaming like she was the sole person responsible for such an event. Maybe she was. Claire wouldn't have met Jake without her.

"Hailey filled us in on the limo ride over," Charlotte said.

The women talked over each other, exclaiming on the double switcheroo with Claire in disguise and the twins switching places.

Claire shrugged. "It worked. Happily so."

"You never told us about your dinner with Joshy," Mad said, poking the strawberry blonde bear.

Hailey flushed bright pink. "Shoot. I left the bean dip in the limo."

"I'll call and have them bring it up," Claire said.

"Is this what you're looking for, Red?" Mad asked, pointing to the insulated cooler slung over Hailey's shoulder.

"Yes!" Hailey exclaimed. "Would you look at that."

"Put it over with the other food," Claire said, gesturing to the bar. "I ordered tamales, enchiladas, taquitos, chips, and guacamole. Oh, and leave room for the best mousse you've ever tasted. There's chocolate and hazelnut."

Hailey and Mad exchanged an excited look and headed over to the food. The other women—Ally, Lauren, Carrie, Charlotte, and Julia—followed quickly behind.

Once they were seated at the table with plates full of food, Claire thanked them for the warm welcome they'd given her. "You all made such a difference in my stay here. I just…I love you guys."

"Awww, Claire!" Hailey exclaimed, jumping up and hugging her.

Mad gave her a high five and the other women all gave her a chorus of "We love you too" that filled her with pure joy.

Claire wiped at her eyes. "We're looking at a release date next December for *Fierce Longing*." She paused and then added casually, "We could watch it together at the premiere in LA."

The women went nuts, hooting and hollering and stomping their feet. Claire exchanged a smile with Julia. She and Julia had recently talked about inviting everyone to the red-carpet event.

Hailey recovered first. "Omigod!" she shrieked. "I can hardly believe we'll be at the premiere. This is so amazing!"

The women chattered excitedly until Hailey finally calmed down enough to say, "Claire, this is truly the highlight of my life. A red-carpet event, that part I played in your movie—"

"A nonspeaking extras role," Claire corrected. She didn't want them to get too carried away. The technical word for extras in a movie was simply *background*, but Claire thought extras sounded nicer, a little more human. Only union actors had speaking parts.

"Which you all played beautifully," Claire added at the unusual silence.

The women smiled back at her with genuine warmth.

"And meeting Blake Grenier," Hailey said. "Even though he's an ass."

Her heart squeezed at the loyalty Hailey showed to her over Blake. "All right, everybody eat. After this, we're heading upstairs to pack up my room. If you find anything in my closet you want for the premiere, it's yours."

Someone gasped.

"For real?" Hailey asked.

Claire laughed. "Yes, for real."

The women went back to eating. Claire listened to the excited chatter about dresses and shoes, happy that she could give them this parting gift.

They finished up the meal, Claire called her contact at the hotel for cleanup and then gestured for the women to follow her out the back door. Frank nodded at them and followed close behind as they headed to the private elevator to her suite. They had to squish into the elevator, all of them strangely silent, smiling at each other and occasionally giggling. Frank stayed in front, facing the doors, stone-faced.

Once Frank gave the all clear that her space was empty of psychos, he left, and the women all filed into her suite. Her friends wandered out of the foyer, gawking. This was the first time she'd invited them to her private space. Though it wouldn't be the last.

"This is what you call your room?" Charlotte asked. "It's an entire hotel floor."

Mad rushed through the rooms in a quick tour. "She even has a dining room!" she hollered.

"You can look around if you want," Claire said to the other women craning their necks to see more of the suite. She trailed after them as the women oohed and aahed over the decor, the luxury appointments, the master bathroom. This was the kind of appreciation she had to remind herself to have. Somehow seeing it through their eyes made it easier to appreciate. When they'd finished, she gestured them toward the master bedroom with the walk-in closet full of her clothes, each item handpicked by her personal shopper. Even on casual days, she had to look put together for the inevitable photo either from a paparazzi or just a fan wanting a selfie with her.

"Mad, you go first," Claire said. "You're about my size. Take your pick of dresses. Anything you want."

Mad flushed bright red. "I'll just watch."

Hailey put her hands on her hips. "What do you mean you'll just watch? Pick something."

Mad traced the carpet with the toe of her black work boot. "I don't know what to pick," she mumbled with an almost shy look.

Claire took in Mad's short disheveled purple hair, her black concert shirt ripped at the collar, and the usual baggy cargo shorts. She remembered Jake telling her about all his brothers and how Mad was one of the guys. Maybe she'd never worn a party dress. Or so rarely that she felt uncomfortable.

Claire started going through her cocktail dresses, looking for the right color for Mad. What went with purple hair, brown eyes, and delicate fair skin? She pulled out a silver sequined dress with a dipping back.

"No," Hailey said. "Purple." She quickly went through the dresses and pulled out two purple dresses, one lavender with a ruffle at the skirt, one a deep purple sleeveless dress that was like a second skin on Claire. It was hard to tell Mad's shape. She guessed her breasts could hold up the sleeveless dress.

"Pick one," Hailey ordered, holding both dresses up to Mad.

Mad lifted her chin. "You pick."

Hailey shoved the dark purple sleeveless one at her. Mad took it with a mumbled, "Thanks." She stood there, holding the dress about a foot away.

"Try it on," Hailey urged.

"Now?" Mad asked. Her cheeks tinged with pink, and she cast a sideways glance at the rest of the women, who weren't even looking at her. They were too busy browsing through Claire's closet.

"Yes, now," Hailey said. "How else are you going to know if it works?"

"I'll do it at home later," Mad mumbled.

Was Mad that shy? Too embarrassed to change in front of the rest of them? Claire never would've guessed it.

Claire crossed to Mad and whispered in her ear, "You can change in the bathroom. I'll keep them busy.

If you don't like the fit, just change back to your regular clothes. But if you do like it, you have to let us see."

Mad nodded once and marched out of the closet.

"Where's she going?" Hailey demanded.

"It's too crowded in here," Claire said. She grabbed the black low-cut dress she'd worn to a charity dinner last spring. "This would look gorgeous with your hair," she told Hailey, handing it to her.

Hailey gasped. "This is Prada!"

"Made especially for me," Claire said.

"Haute couture," Hailey whispered reverently. She turned. "Unzip me." For as long as she'd known Hailey, she was always in a dress.

Claire unzipped her. Hailey stepped out of her dress and slipped the other one over her head. Claire did the tiny clasp across the waist in back for her.

Hailey preened. "Omigod! I love it!" She went to the mirror and did a little twirl. Then she rushed at Claire, throwing her arms around her. "Thank you!"

Claire's eyes misted as she hugged her back. "You're quite welcome."

Hailey browsed the shoe racks next, trying on several pairs, and then picked a pair of black Versace stilettos with gold-covered heels. She beamed at Claire. "They're a little tight, but I'll make them work."

"I'll get something in your size," Claire said.

"You're probably going to be wearing them all night for the premiere and the after party."

Hailey made a comical jaw drop at that. Claire laughed.

Hailey turned to the group, who were still shopping in Claire's closet. "Ladies! What do you think?" She posed, one hand on her hip.

"Wow," Ally said in a hushed whisper. The group fell silent, mouths agape, as all eyes went past Hailey to where Mad stood self-consciously, legs shoulder-width apart in an aggressive stance. She'd left her boots behind. Without her usual armor, she looked petite and feminine. Stunning, actually. Except for her snarly face.

"What?" Mad snapped. "What're you all staring at?"

"It's perfect," Claire said. "You look beautiful."

Mad's expression softened. "Oh."

The women gathered around Mad, fussing over her new look, making Mad squirm and blush before she finally barked, "Okay, okay! It's not that big a deal. Now I need shoes. All I have are sneakers and boots."

Claire looked at her feet, petite and slender. "Size six?" she guessed.

Mad pointed at her. "She's good."

Claire grabbed Mad's hand and pulled her over to the shoe racks.

Hailey appeared at her side. "This collection is amazing!"

Mad stared at the designer shoes ranging from stilettos to pumps to strappy sandals. "Pick something for me," she told Hailey.

Hailey was delighted, picking up each shoe with reverence and announcing the designer and season to everyone. The woman was a true shoe aficionado. After several minutes of Hailey putting on the greatest shoe show known to earth, Mad finally snapped. "Would you just pick one? I need to get back into my regular clothes. This dress is tight."

Hailey narrowed her eyes. "It's not tight. It fits you perfectly. You're just used to walking around in a sack."

Mad didn't take offense. "Sacks are very comfortable."

Hailey looked her up and down before settling on a black pair of Louboutin stilettos. "Try them on. Carefully. These are three-thousand-dollar shoes."

"Get out!" Mad exclaimed. "No one pays that much for shoes."

Hailey jabbed her finger at the shoes.

Mad turned to Claire, eyes wide. "Seriously? You pay that much for this tiny piece of shoe? My boots cost fifty bucks with a lot more material, and they're made to last."

"Don't you know anything about women's fashion?" Hailey asked.

Mad crossed her arms. "Sorry, Red, I didn't spend my childhood poring over women's fashion mags."

"Your mom never took you shopping?" Hailey asked.

"Don't remember my mom," Mad muttered. She shoved her feet into the stilettos and wobbled for a moment, grabbing Hailey's arm for balance. "How the fuck do you walk in these?"

"Practice," Claire said.

Hailey nodded. "Did your mom, um, pass on?"

"Nah," Mad said. "She's still alive and kicking somewhere. Least I think she is. I'd probably hear something otherwise. Who needs her? I had ten big brothers and a great dad to make up for her." She pounded a fist against her chest. "Found Boys. Never surrender."

Found Boys plus a girl, Claire thought. Mad didn't seem to realize she'd referred to herself as a boy.

"Ten big brothers?" Charlotte exclaimed. "That's intense."

"Five biological brothers and five brothers from another mother," Mad said, perking up. "I'm the youngest. It was like having an entire baseball team looking out for me." She jutted her chin out. "Now I look out for myself."

"Boy, were you outnumbered," Hailey said.

The women murmured sympathetically and gazed at Mad with new understanding in their eyes.

Mad took a practice walk, tottering on the heels. "No big. It was awesome. Still is." She twisted an ankle, ripped off the shoe and flung it.

Hailey gasped. "You did *not* just throw a Louboutin!"

Mad scowled at the shoe and pulled the other one off. "Stupid shoe made me twist an ankle. I've got flag football on turkey day with my brothers." She winced and walked it off, limping out of the closet and down the hallway.

Hailey retrieved the shoe sitting against one of Claire's crushed velvet boots and looked it over carefully. Mad returned, and Hailey held the shoe up to her. "You're lucky there's no damage."

"Almost damaged me," Mad returned.

Claire went to the shoe racks and pulled out another pair of black heels, Jimmy Choos, with a chunky heel. "Try these." She placed them on the floor next to Mad, who was testing out her ankle by bending and jumping like she was shooting a basketball.

"Ankle's good," Mad said.

Hailey pointed to the shoes. Mad shoved her feet in them.

"Carefully!" Hailey admonished. She shook her head as Mad grabbed her arm for balance again. "That's why you dress like a guy. You don't know how to be a girl."

"Fuck you!" Mad snapped, jerking away from Hailey. "I know how to be a girl!"

The room fell silent.

Hailey immediately tried to backtrack. "I'm sorry. I just, I didn't know…" She trailed off at Mad's hostile glare. "I can help you."

"I don't need help!" Mad barked.

Hailey and Mad had a staredown. Hailey's gaze went from defensive to empathetic in a snap. Mad jutted her chin out, her belligerent expression back in place.

"My turn!" Ally announced, breaking the tension. "I'd like something in blue."

Claire hurried to help Ally, and the women soon focused on getting each of them fitted.

Hailey walked Mad up and down the long stretch between the bedroom and kitchenette in the heels, all while distracting her with questions about her brothers and her favorite sports teams. It was Hailey's subtle way of teaching Mad to walk in heels. She occasionally tossed in instructions—keep your head up, one foot in front of the other, no shuffling, heel to toe in a smooth rolling motion. By the time Mad returned to the closet where all of them were in dresses, Mad was beaming.

"I totally rock this dress-shoe combo," Mad said.

"All my beauty pageant training really came through," Hailey exclaimed proudly.

Mad curled her lip. "Pageants are bogus."

"Be glad for it," Hailey said, bumping Mad with her hip.

"Better watch it, Red, I'm a fourth-degree black belt. You'll be kissing the ground in two seconds flat."

Hailey studied Mad for a moment. "Maybe we'll get you kissing someone soon."

Mad snorted indelicately. "Sorry. Don't think you can set me up with your go-to guy."

Everyone laughed. Hailey's go-to guy was Mad's brother Josh. At least he was before he hit number one on Hailey's shit list. The poor man would never date in that town again if Hailey had anything to say about it.

"Anyone catch your eye?" Hailey asked.

Mad went scarlet. "No!"

The women laughed. There was someone.

"Maddy has a crush," Hailey sang.

Mad marched out of the closet, and then turned back to holler, "It's Mad and get a life!"

Hailey smiled sweetly. "I have a very nice life because of wonderful friends like you."

Mad blinked a few times, her eyes shiny as she

stumbled back into the room on tottering heels. "Shut up, Red. Payback's a bitch."

Hailey threw an arm over Mad's shoulders and leaned her head against Mad's.

Claire shook her head with a smile. "I need a picture of this." She looked at her friends, all dressed up, beautiful inside and out. "Actually I need pictures of all of you. Come on."

They headed to the living room and took a series of photos with her cell phone—posing like models, funny faces, and her favorite, all of them crowded in together, arms around each other in one giant squeezy hug, hollering, "SLUTS forever!"

But, of course, they all knew they were in it for the happy ending.

~ ~ ~

Late the next day, Claire arrived at Jake's gorgeous contemporary home. She asked Frank to wait in the car, needing to see Jake on her own. For some reason, she was nervous.

And then she saw him, barefoot in jeans and a T-shirt, striding toward the door. He opened it and grinned. "Hi, neighbor."

"Hi," she said over the lump in her throat.

He pulled her inside, his arms wrapping around her. She let out a sigh, surrounded by warmth and love. Her long journey through this past hellish month had all been to bring her to this moment, this final stop, to find Jake again.

He pulled back and cradled her face with both hands. "Move in with me."

Her lips parted in surprise, even though she really wanted to. She never wanted to leave him again. "You should get to know me better—"

"Do you have any idea what it's like to finally feel like…" He dropped his hands and rubbed his chest. "I had this empty ache. Nothing could fill it, not work, not parties, nothing, and then you came along and it was like I could breathe again. Do you know how rare that is?"

She bit her lip and nodded. "I do." She rubbed his chest, remembering her own ever-present ache of loneliness. It was filled now with true friends and true love. "I feel the same way."

He covered her hand, holding it against him. "And it's not because of your name. I liked Jenny plenty, and when I found out who you really were, I didn't care about your movie star shine because it was you, the real you, playing around with me and fighting with me and hooking up with me, even when you wore a red wig and strangely green contacts."

She laughed. "Make love. It sounds nicer than hook up."

He smiled and gave her a smacking kiss on the lips. "Yes. Sorry, guy talk. Short answer is, I liked Jenny, I love Claire."

She wrapped her arms around his neck and kissed him, her heart soaring at the words she felt soul deep. "I love you too."

"Good. Now that we got that out of the way. Is Frank living with us too?"

She laughed. "He stays at a guesthouse on the property. I need him. It's not just autographs fans want from me. I found a strange man naked in my bed, reciting lines from one of my movies, trying to get me to join him. Men try to grab me—*mrwmph*."

He'd pressed her tight against his chest, his hand cupping the back of her head in a protective hold. "My God, Claire, I had no idea. We're keeping him. Maybe you should have two Franks."

"One is plenty." He loosened his hold, and she lifted her head. "He's former Army Special Forces. Nothing gets past him."

"Okay." He dipped his head, meeting her eyes. "I don't want to hide from the press. I want to be a normal couple."

"Normal isn't in my future. But, how about this, we'll fly under the radar for a month, and then, after you've been briefed on the Claire Jordan protocol, you can take a baby step out there."

"Oh, the Claire Jordan protocol, huh?"

She grinned. "Yeah. It's not as easy as it looks to have the spotlight on you. It's harsh, intrusive, and unforgiving."

He shifted, pressing his lips to the side of her neck, gliding hot kisses up to her ear. "I'm tough. Screw those judgmental gossip rags. As long as I have you."

"You do," she said on a sigh.

He met her eyes. "So that's what I'm promising you. Totally cool with cameras and all that shit. Here's what I want from you. A solemn promise. Put that hand up."

She put her hand up with a laugh. "Is this where I swear on a Bible?"

He took her hand and placed it over his heart. "You swear right here. You will remember how much I love you and never put the press and what they might say above us."

Her eyes got hot. "Jake, I wouldn't—"

"Swear it, Claire."

"I swear. I know I got really worked up—"

"Really, really worked up."

"Yes," she said dryly. "Really, really worked up over the movie buzz. I had a good reason."

"But…"

"But that was before I fell in love with the amazing Jake Campbell."

He grabbed her wrist and lifted her arm in the air. "The lady wins a prize!" He kissed her and spoke against her lips. "Me."

She laughed. "Dork."

"You're going to be calling me a very different name in a few short minutes."

"Oh really?" she said, her smile big and beaming. This man. He really was amazing and confident enough to hold up under the scrutiny she knew they'd have to endure.

His arm wrapped around her waist, walking her back to the wall. "Yes, really," he said with an unholy gleam in his dark eyes.

Her back hit the wall, and Jake pressed against her front. His fingers speared through her hair, tilting her head for his kiss. She met his deep brown eyes, felt as much as saw the love shining in them. "I missed you so much," she whispered.

His lips grazed hers. "I missed you too much."

They gazed at each other, lost in the wonder of it all. Then they slammed together in a furious frenzy of kissing and stripping of clothes until they were joined together as one.

Joined together in love.

Joined together for life.

EPILOGUE

After a passionate month of living together, they went public, dating in the spotlight. Jake still found it annoying, the intrusion into their private moments, but Claire taught him a lot about grace under pressure, about making the press feel like they got something important from her (when they got only what she chose to give), and how to keep the public separate from the private. The buzz was on them as the adorable "it" couple, nicknamed Jaire, and that was okay because he had the woman of his dreams.

His investment in *Fierce Longing*'s marketing campaign had paid off big time, as he fully expected it would. Blake had caught on quick the direction things were going for the big movie release and went out of his way to gush over Claire and the Fierce movies. Opening night tickets had sold out three months in advance for the December release.

Now they were walking the red carpet for the

movie premiere, a barrier wall on one side of them, security and more barriers on the other, the flash of cameras nearly blinding him. Blake went first with his hot model date followed by the Happy Endings Book Club members, and then Jake, Claire, and an unobtrusively hovering Frank. Jake had a whole new appreciation for Frank once Claire told him all of her horror stories of aggressive and, frankly, nutso fans.

Hailey waved and smiled at some screaming Fierce fanatics, hamming it up for the cameras and holding up her signed copy of *Fierce Longing*. She claimed credit for him and Claire getting together and had been lobbying to plan the wedding ever since their secret engagement (need-to-know basis), but he and Claire wanted something private. It would be at an undisclosed time in an undisclosed location with invites going out only two weeks in advance to a select few, including his family and closest friends, her family, and the book club. Truth was, they'd been waiting for the holidays and the return of his blood brother Parker Shaw. Park was heading home, for good, now that his air force service was up.

Mad elbowed Hailey, and they had a brief harsh discussion. Those two, surprisingly enough considering their differences, had become close. Mad had let Hailey glam her up with hair and makeup for tonight's event, but insisted on a pants suit instead of a dress. Next to all the other dresses of the book club women, his sister stood out even more than she normally would with her dyed fire-engine red hair.

"Claire! Claire! Over here!" reporters shouted.

Claire stopped at the turn in the carpet in front of the theater, smiling and shifting subtly in her shimmering silver gown while the cameras went off. Jake let go of her hand so she could do her thing, and just watched her, lit up, gracious, laughing. He found himself smiling what was probably a goofy lovesick smile, but he didn't care. It was real, and he'd never been so happy.

They went into the theater to watch her movie together for the first time. Julia, the famously reclusive author, had a private viewing of the movie at home. Claire didn't even try to get her out to LA because Julia was all gaga for her newborn daughter, Grace. He and Claire would be starting a family just as soon as she wrapped the Fierce trilogy.

After they took their seats, he whispered in his fiancée's ear, "I want a repeat performance of any and all simulated sex scenes in this movie, Mrs. Jake Campbell."

She smiled, and turned to him, eyes bright. He loved that "Mrs. Jake Campbell" always made her smile. Though it wasn't official yet, he'd been calling her that ever since he proposed. To the public she would always be Claire Jordan. That was a bankable brand that would keep going as long as she wanted.

He grinned and added, "You owe me that for watching you with this homely pretend lover." He gestured at the screen. Never mind that Blake had just been named Sexiest Man Alive. It was Jake who'd pushed to make him so. All part of the Fierce movie marketing campaign. If the fans couldn't have Claire and Blake together, they could obsess over Blake and imagine themselves with him. Win-win.

"I don't think so," she said in a teasing voice.

"And why not?"

"Everything we do is one hundred percent real. No simulations, no pretending."

He brought her hand to his lips and grazed her knuckles. "Yes."

She quirked a brow, a devilish gleam in those hazel eyes. "Besides, I'm not sure you can take it to this level of alpha."

"Oh, it is *on*."

They gazed into each other's eyes, grinning like idiots.

The theater lights dimmed. He gave her a quick kiss and settled in for what he was sure was the first of many movie premieres. He still owned Dat Cloud, but he'd cut back his hours, taking more time off to travel with Claire. She was at the top of her game, and he was all in for wherever the ride took them. They'd settle down, eventually, and raise a family, but for now it was all about the next big opportunity. He liked the business side of her production company and had launched a massive online advertising campaign and a slick website.

The movie title, *Fierce Longing*, flashed on the screen, and he knew what those words meant on a heart level. That longing to fill the empty ache of loneliness deep inside. Something he and Claire had both felt before they found each other. And he knew soul deep what the final installment, *Fierce Loving*, meant too. To love wholly, completely, fiercely. Forever.

~THE END~

Dear Readers,

What do you think about Hailey and Josh? Will they or won't they? I think they're enjoying the frenemy thing too much to stop. LOL You know who really needs a happy ending? Mad Campbell. That tough chick has a secretly mushy heart for the man she worshipped as a teen. Would you like an exclusive sneak peek at my next release? Just sign up for my newsletter at www.kyliegilmore.com/newsletter, and you'll receive sneak peeks, excerpts, and subscriber-only giveaways. Next up is Mad Campbell's story, *Inviting Trouble*, book 2 in the Happy Endings Book Club series. Join the club and get your happy ending!

Inviting Trouble (Happy Endings Book Club #2)
She's always been one of the guys...

Raised in an all-male household, Madison "Mad" Campbell was once proud to be a tomboy. Until she developed a hard case of lust for her older brother's crazy hot friend Parker Shaw. And maybe he noticed her too because he was the only one in the testosterone-addled bunch to include her instead of sending her away. One drunken kiss—that he has no memory of—is all she has before Park leaves for the

Air Force.

He's never been a prince…

Parker was a lost boy, heading down a dark path, until he met the Campbell boys who became like family. Not only did they help him through a tumultuous childhood, they gave him the little sister experience. Mad has always been off-limits, a point driven home by his best friend Ty Campbell, which was no problem until he realized her boy clothes were hiding a future knock out. One kiss tells him he's reached the limits of his control.

She's making some big changes…

Parker is back, sexier than ever, and Mad is determined to show Park she's all grown up and more than capable of handling him. So why is she trembling at the thought? What insanity made her cave to a makeover from the meddling matchmaker in charge of The Happy Endings Book Club?

Sign up for my newsletter to be notified when the second book, *Inviting Trouble*, releases at www. kyliegilmore.com.

Also by Kylie Gilmore

The Clover Park Series

THE OPPOSITE OF WILD (Book 1)
DAISY DOES IT ALL (Book 2)
BAD TASTE IN MEN (Book 3)
KISSING SANTA (Book 4)
RESTLESS HARMONY (Book 5)
NOT MY ROMEO (Book 6)
REV ME UP (Book 7)
AN AMBITIOUS ENGAGEMENT (Book 8)
CLUTCH PLAYER (Book 9)
A TEMPTING FRIENDSHIP (Book 10)

The Clover Park STUDS Series

ALMOST IN LOVE (Book 1)
ALMOST MARRIED (Book 2)
ALMOST OVER IT (Book 3)
ALMOST ROMANCE (Book 4)
ALMOST HITCHED (Book 5)

Happy Endings Book Club Series

HIDDEN HOLLYWOOD (Book 1)

Acknowledgments

Thanks to you! Yes, you, dear romance reader, for inspiring the Happy Endings Book Club! Because wouldn't it be great to dish with other avid romance readers? Thanks also to my family, Tessa, Pauline, Paul, Mimi, Kim, and Jenn for all you do. Thanks to my readers group, the Gilmore Goddesses, for cheering me on! Join us at facebook.com/groups/GilmoreGoddesses, all reader goddesses are welcome!

About the Author

Kylie Gilmore is the *USA Today* bestselling author of the Happy Endings Book Club series, the Clover Park series, and the Clover Park STUDS series. She writes quirky, tender romance with a solid dose of humor.

Kylie lives in New York with her family, two cats, and a nutso dog. When she's not writing, wrangling kids, or dutifully taking notes at writing conferences, you can find her flexing her muscles all the way to the high cabinet for her secret chocolate stash.

Praise for Kylie Gilmore

THE OPPOSITE OF WILD

"This book is everything a reader hopes for. Funny. Hot. Sweet."
—New York Times Bestselling Author, Mimi Jean Pamfiloff

"It's intriguing and complex while still being light hearted and truly romantic. To see a male so twisted and turned is unusual but honestly made the book all the more enjoyable."
—Harlequin Junkie

"Ms. Gilmore's writing style draws the reader in and does not let go until the very end of the story and leaves you wanting more."
—Romance Bookworm

"Every aspect of this novel touched me and left me unable to put it down. I pulled an all-nighter, staying up until after 3 am to get to the last page."
—Luv Books Galore

DAISY DOES IT ALL

"The characters in this book are downright hilarious sometimes. I mean, when you start a book off with a fake life and immediately follow it by a rejected proposal, you know that you are in for a fun ride."
—The Little Black Book Blog

"Daisy Does It All is a sweet book with a hint of sizzle. The characters are all very real and I found myself laughing along with them and also having my heart ripped in two for them."
—A is for Alpha, B is for Book

BAD TASTE IN MEN

"I gotta dig a friends to lovers story, and Ms. Gilmore's 3rd book in the Clover Park Series hits the spot. A great dash of humor, a few pinches of steam, and a whole lotta love...Gilmore has won me over with everything I've read and she's on my auto buy list...she's on my top list of new authors for 2014."
—Storm Goddess Book Reviews

"The chemistry between the two characters is so real and so intense, it will have you turning the pages into the midnight hour. Throw in a bit of comedy – a dancing cow, a sprained ankle, and a bit of jealousy and Gilmore has a recipe for great success."
—Underneath the Covers blog

KISSING SANTA

"I love that Samantha and Rico are set up by none other than their mothers. And the journey they go on is really hilarious!! I laughed out loud so many times, my kids asked me what was wrong with me."
—Amazeballs Book Addicts

"I absolutely adored this read. It was quick, funny, sexy and got me in the Christmas spirit. Samantha and Rico are a great couple that keep one another all riled up in more ways than one, and their sexual tension is super hot."
—Read, Tweet, Repeat

RESTLESS HARMONY

"Kylie's writing as usual is full of laugh out loud humor, touching moments, and heat that will make you fan yourself... If you are looking for a book that will having you laughing out loud and feeling good when you are done, this book is for you."
—Smut and Bonbons blog

"My heart broke for Gabe's past, but it soared for the understanding and love in which he got through from a family born of true love and commitment. Kylie brought the real with this one. Heartache, love, support, sexiness, and beliefs."
—Reading by the Book blog

NOT MY ROMEO

"Their sexual tension and continuous banter had me smiling. I couldn't get enough and stayed up late just to finish their story, because I had to know where it went."
—Book Junky Girls blog

"They may not have been Romeo and Juliet, but they sure made one hell of a story that kept me laughing and reading on."
—Smut and Bonbons blog

REV ME UP

"The way Lily and Nico met cracked me up. Let's just say it was a wild case of mistaken identity! It pulled me in and I couldn't put the book down!"
—Romance Novel Giveaways blog

"It was a mission to make the sexy 'wrong' redhead see how wonderful and lovable she really was. It was giving her the family she desired and longed for. It was Clover Park series perfection. Love. Italian wedding cookies. Unity. Forever."
—Reading by the Book blog

"Rev Me Up is a heartwarming fun read. Kylie infuses her sense of humor in the heroine that I always enjoy reading and the men in Clover Park make me want to pay it a visit!"
—Smut and Bonbons blog

ALMOST IN LOVE

"Ms. Gilmore is an excellent storyteller, and her main characters are hard to forget, but her secondary characters are equally impressive. This is a character-driven tale inside of a sweet plot to get two nice people to fall in love and have their HEA."
—*USA Today*, Happy Ever After blog

"Forget alpha-male billionaires. The Studs will have you panting for that guy in nerdy glasses."
—New York Times Bestselling Author, Mimi Jean Pamfiloff

"I was pulled in quickly and between the fascinating characters, the witty banter, the flow of the story and the emotions I was feeling I was blown away! I loved every second."
—A Beautiful Book blog

Thanks!

Thanks for reading *Hidden Hollywood*. I hope you enjoyed it. Would you like to know about new releases? You can sign up for my new release email list at kyliegilmore.com/newsletter. I promise not to clog your inbox! Only new release info and some fun giveaways. You can also sign up by scanning this QR code:

I love to hear from readers! You can find me at:
kyliegilmore.com
Facebook.com/KylieGilmoreToo
Twitter @KylieGilmoreToo

If you liked Jake and Claire's story, please leave a review on your favorite retailer's website or Goodreads. Thank you!

Made in the USA
Columbia, SC
17 February 2018